MW00880917

TODAY & TOMORROW

T A PERRET

Today
&
Tomorrow

Holly Springs Book 2
A Novel by T.A. Perret

Dedication
To my mom - you always told me to go after my dreams
but try not to hurt anyone on the way.
I hope I have made you proud.
I love you.

PREMISE

A false witness will not go unpunished, and he who
breathes out lies will perish.
Proverbs 19:9 (ESV)

Casting my gaze downward, I nervously pick at my nail polish and notice dirt underneath two broken nails. A few short hours ago, my perfectly manicured nails matched the dress I had worn. I'm no longer confident Tomorrow Williams, the senior class president at Holly Springs High. The girl in the reflection is a stranger to me.

THE HOMECOMING DANCE should be over by now. My twin sister, Today, will be home soon. Just once, I hope she'll go straight to her room instead of checking how my night had been. Today is my older twin sister by twelve minutes. She was born on a Tuesday at 11:54 p.m.; I was born on Wednesday at 12:06 a.m. Our mom thought it would be clever to name her identical twins Today and Tomorrow.

At seventeen, we share everything—clothes, makeup, a Volkswagen we call Cricket since a belt chirped when Dad bought her for us, and of course, secrets. We always share secrets. Tales of first kisses, first dates, when one cheated on a history test in the ninth grade, and when the other one admitted she and her best friend smoked a cigarette. We tell each other everything. Up until tonight, that is. Tonight, I'll keep the biggest secret of my life from my sister and lie to her for the first time ever. She enters my room without knocking, as usual.

"How was your night? I didn't see you at the dance," Today asks, oblivious to my red-rimmed, puffy eyes. "Troy took forever to meet me at the dance. He gave some flimsy excuse about running into an old friend and lost track of time." She rolls her eyes and says, "We didn't stay long once he arrived, so I probably just missed you." She giggles and plops down on the bed beside me. Troy Whitaker is Today's "forever boyfriend," as she calls him. They have been dating since their first year of high school. She hugs an overstuffed black pillow; I can tell her mind has drifted back to the evening with Troy. Strands of her deep auburn hair fall from her updo, framing her face and giving her a whimsical windswept look. Her slightly flushed, freckled cheeks make her emerald eyes sparkle. I know by looking at my twin that she had a great time. *Such irony*, I think to myself. Today is glowing, and my inner candle has been blown out.

"Fine," I reply flatly, fidgeting with the charm bracelet my parents gave me when I was baptized two years earlier. It's the one piece of jewelry I never take off. I try looking Today in the eye, but the shame washes over me again. I have a knot in the pit of my stomach, and my hands tremble. I tuck them under my legs, hoping she isn't paying attention. "I didn't go to the dance. I wasn't feeling well. Besides, I didn't have a date." I don't want to discuss this right now. I want to go to bed.

"Fine? What does that mean? And I thought you were going with Caleb." She studies me closely, making me feel uncomfortable. I need to get her out of my room and soon. Otherwise, the entire mess will come pouring out like a broken levy. "What's going on, Tomorrow? I can tell something is wrong."

"Nothing. And you know Caleb and I are only friends." I stammer and plaster on the most genuine smile I can muster. "I'm just tired and still not feeling well. We'll talk in the morning before I go to work, okay?" I'm exhausted and want this conversation to end. Now.

"Okay, deal," she exclaims and pops off my bed. "Oh, and by the way, I know better about Caleb." She winks and giggles again. Today's bubbly personality and enthusiasm for life are two of her greatest assets. I, on the other hand, can't keep up with her effervescence, even on a good day. I'm the wallflower of the two of us. I envy her for that. Mom always points out that we both got the better end of the stick. I've never figured out how that's possible. Today kisses me on the cheek and bounces towards the door. "Night, Morrow Bear."

"Goodnight, Taddy Day," I reply, but she is already gone.

I hear my look-alike roaming around in her room, getting ready for bed. I can hear her humming to a pop tune streaming from her Alexa, which comforts me. Normalcy is what I need. I also need to rewind the clock to yesterday and make life normal again.

Mom and Dad have already turned in for the night, and it's reassuring that I'm not the only one awake in the house. Twenty minutes later, though, the music stops, and I hear the light switch click off next door. In the stillness of my room, I hear a light rapping on the wall beside my bed, the wall that separates our bedrooms. One tap. Three taps. One tap. I listen to our childhood Morse code for "I luv U." I reply with two taps of my own. "I luv U, too."

Once Today has gone to bed, the silence is deafening as I lay back on my bed again. Depression and gloom surround me, engulfing me in a thick black fog. I watch the numbers on my bedside clock flip over, one by one. The darkness is too much for me to deal with. Every time I close my eyes, his face appears behind my lids. Reaching across my night-stand, I flip the lamp on; the brightness filling the dark corners of my room makes me feel safer.

I stare at the picture frame on my nightstand. It's my favorite photo of Faith, our older sister, Today, and myself at the beach last summer. We appear so happy in our matching yellow polka-dot bikinis, big floppy sun hats, and sunglasses. We look so much alike that only our family can tell us apart—same wavy red hair, same green eyes. The only difference is that I have a diamond stud piercing in my nose. We probably even have the same number of freckles on our cheeks. We can pass for triplets, but Faith is a year older. I sigh and lay the picture face down on the night-stand. Happy isn't a feeling I can conjure right now. Even with the lights on, staring at my ceiling, I can hear him breathing in my ear, smell the beer on his breath, and feel his hands touching me. I shiver under the covers and begin to cry again.

I roll over in my bed and dig deeper into the soft security of my duvet. I am cradled in softness. Warm and cozy, I float into that half-dream state where nothing matters—finally getting some relief from the mental anguish I've been experiencing for the past several hours.

Before I know it, my alarm clock blares. Loud, obnoxious ringing bells insist on becoming my reality. The rudeness of the alarm alerts me that I'll be late for work if I don't get moving. I want to call in sick, but I can't do that to my boss and co-workers. They're like a second family, and Caleb will ask a ton of questions. I have the early shift this morning with him at Thanks A Latte, the small, upbeat coffee shop where I've worked since my sophomore year at HSHS. My shift is scheduled to start in fifteen minutes. Crap!

Sprinting from my bed, I dash into my bathroom for another shower. I still want to call in sick, but I know I'm needed. I still feel dirty, but this shower has to be super quick. When the hot water cascades down my naked body, the memories of last night flood my brain again. Reliving every touch, sound, smell, and word spoken is too much. The tears begin flowing freely. I wonder if I will ever stop crying.

Today and I share a Jack-and-Jill bathroom connecting our bedrooms. Knocking at the door, my twin asks, "Morrow, are you crying?" I hear the concern in her voice. Hiding behind the shower curtain, I struggle to pull myself together.

"Yes, I'm fine. I was...singing." My chuckle is so fake that I cringe. "My singing must be pretty bad if you thought I was crying." My voice comes across too high-pitched to be believable. I pray she misses the sorrow I'm trying to hide. Today is the last person I can talk to about last night. It would hurt her almost as much as me if she knew what happened.

Still reeling from my shattered nerves, I turn off the water, wrap myself in a fluffy white towel, and prepare to see my sister face-to-face.

I pad across the white carpet barefoot, and duck into my

walk-in closet to get dressed. I can't do it. I can't bring myself
to look at my sister. With one glance, she will know something is terribly wrong.

"Hand me that black skirt on the chair," I say to her in a
much cheerier tone than I feel. I pull on a white short-
sleeved blouse, the black skirt she hands me, and a cute pair
of Mary Janes. I am almost ready to try to face the world.
"Almost" is the operative word. Sitting at my dressing table, I
stare back at the girl in the mirror. Her eyes are dull, and her
lips turn downward. A touch of mascara and some lip gloss
help very little. She's damaged goods. That's what I am now.
Today stands behind me, studying me in the mirror. I give
her a quick smile, but that does nothing to diminish my
sadness, and I look away.

"Here, let me French braid your hair before you go," she
says sweetly, gently squeezing my shoulders. We would take
turns fixing each other's hair when we were younger. Today
is the master at intricate braids, and I can do wonders with a
curling iron. I'm tearful as I recount the many hours we
spent surfing the internet for new styling techniques. I
quickly wipe away a rogue tear before it escapes, and I stand
to go.

"Time to go. I'm so late. Vickie is going to kill me," I state,
exasperated as I glance at my watch. I need to go before she
notices I'm on the verge of a breakdown. I wonder if this will
be the norm for me from now on; devoid of all emotion,
except sadness and shame. I feel flat. I can't even look at
Today, much less talk to her. Isolated in my memories of hell
on Earth, this is the loneliest I have ever felt. I collect my
purse and cell phone, and turn on my heel to leave.

"Morrow Bear, what's wrong? I can tell something is
bothering you." Her brows knit in concern. I never can get
anything past her. "Don't even try to lie to me. I always know

when you are lying. So, fess up," she demands, arms akimbo, fully expecting a response. That's not going to happen. Not today. Not ever.

I fiddle with the purity ring on my right hand and whisper, "I have to go." With that, I escape from my bedroom, tears streaming down my cheeks again.

2

W alking into Thanks A Latte, Taylor Swift croons from the sound system. I've never been a big fan of hers, but the high school and college crowd like her. "Whatever keeps them coming back," my boss, Vickie, the owner of Thanks A Latte, always says. *Only eight hours,* I think. *I can do anything for eight hours.* I can't wait to get home and back in bed.

The coffee shop isn't busy yet, and relief washes over me. The morning rush of older adults has already subsided, and it's too early for the college kids to be out of bed. But I know it won't be long before the line is stretched to the door. I always love coming here, especially on Saturday mornings. The aroma of brewing coffee and pastries would be my perfume of choice, if only I could figure out how to bottle it. It's my second home. I've been known to hold Student Council meetings here occasionally. Oversized windows line the front of the shop. Vickie went all out and added cute little dinette tables and chairs covered in coffee cup motif linens. The coffee shop has plenty of seating, modern light fixtures hanging from the ceiling, and a trendy gift section right at the front of the store that gives a comfortable vibe to the space. The walls are decorated with an eclectic display of paintings and artwork done by local artists that can be purchased by the public. It's Vickie's way of promoting rising artists; she doesn't charge to display anybody's work and give back to Holly Springs. Most of it's pretty good. Behind the counter is an assortment of coffee machines, latte machines, and the like. A large display case highlights Vickie's love of baking. *"Coffee and sweets keep the world in motion"* is painted on the wall as the focal point of the coffee house. My plan is to duck into the bathroom to fix my makeup before anyone spots me. My plan fails miserably.

"Hey Tater Bug, keeping bankers' hours now?" Caleb Logan, my best friend since second grade, announces my tardy arrival to everyone in the shop, including our boss. Vickie glances up from her supply order sheet and peers over her red reading glasses. She quirks an eyebrow but says nothing.

"It's not like you to be late. Now, your sister, on the other hand, is another story completely," he continues. "Are you sure you aren't Today covering, so your sister can head to the lake?" Caleb laughs at his own joke. At least he thinks he's funny. Typically, I would join in and tease him, since he is usually the late one and never me. Not today, though. I'm definitely not feeling it.

"I overslept," I say, dashing into the restroom in the back.

I splash cool water on my face to reduce the puffiness around my eyes and assess the damage of the freshly fallen tears. Thanks to waterproof mascara, I don't look too bad. Patting my face dry, I apply fresh lip gloss and a touch of concealer beneath my eyes. It helps tone down the red blotches. I can't go out there looking like I've been crying, which is precisely the case. I don't bother covering the freckles on my cheeks and nose because no amount of concealer will keep them hidden. Before opening the door, I take one last glance in the mirror and inhale a deep cleansing breath, allowing the familiar smells of the shop to comfort me; freshly ground coffee beans, muffins baking in the oven, and vanilla wafting through the air. I'm comforted for the time being.

"OH, MY GOD," I gasp. Caleb is standing on the other side of the door, hand raised to knock, when I open the door. "You scared me to death," I exclaim, placing my hand on my chest to calm my racing heart. I quickly step away from him.

"Sorry, Morrow. I came to check on you. You didn't look so good when you came in," he informs me. Gazing down at his feet, he shifts his weight from one foot to the other. "Is something wrong?" he says, sounding worried. My heart breaks a little. Caleb always watches out for me. He's my rock.

How many times have I been asked that in the past eighteen hours? I need to get better control of my emotions. I bite my lower lip to keep it from quivering. If there is anybody on this planet that I trust enough to tell what happened, it's Caleb. That's out of the question, though. It's too embarrassing and shameful. I should have been able to stop this from happening last night. I push the memory down as best I can. Shame is now my constant companion, and I fear everyone can see it.

"No, I'm fine, just flushed from trying to get here so fast in this heat. I was late, remember?" I jab at him sarcastically. *Fake it until you make it,* I think to myself. I've heard that line somewhere before; I can't remember where, but that's what I must do. Fake it until I make it. "You made sure to point that out to Vickie," I quirked up at him. "What's up with this heat, anyway?" I ask, exasperated, and breeze past him in the narrow hallway before he can answer or ask any more questions. I grab my apron and take my place behind the counter.

Business picks up almost immediately, leaving little time for conversation with Caleb. I'm thankful. Keeping my mind busy is helpful as I can get lost in my work, making the morning fly by. I love working at the coffee shop. I meet new people, but regular customers come in almost daily for their usual caffeine fixes. I find myself messing up and forgetting drink orders I can normally recite in my sleep. Caleb keeps thumping me on my head every time I mess up. I've always prided myself on remembering names, faces, and coffee orders. Today, I'm totally off my game.

"Do you need more caffeine this morning or something, Tater?" he asks teasingly, but I catch the flash of concern in his deep green eyes. Even though my memory is failing me this morning, it feels good to be among friends.

"No, perfect barista boy. I need a large, non-fat mocha frappé with a shot, no whip. Please. K? Thanks," I shoot in his direction and wink at the brunette who placed the order. She comes in daily, a Thanks A Latte junkie, so it's okay not to be entirely professional. "Oh, and I need that on the double." She chuckles at the banter between Caleb and I.

"You two are so cute together," she says and smiles sweetly. "Why do you call her Tater, though?" she inquires.

Caleb begins to tell his favorite story, which is about my nickname. "We were in elementary school, and they served sweet potatoes for lunch one afternoon. You know, healthy food and all. Tomorrow held up the potato and said, 'There is something wrong with this potato. It's the same color as my hair! I'm not eating this!' I had to explain it was a sweet potato, like her. From then on, I call her Tater Bug or Tater, 'cause that's what she is." He loves embarrassing me with that story.

"You make the perfect couple," she states with a dreamy gaze in her eyes.

"Oh, no. We aren't..." I sputter as Caleb cuts in.

"Aren't we, though?" he teases, flashing a dazzling smile. He places the order on the counter and heads in the opposite direction. I laugh self-consciously but find myself admiring how he looks in those jeans. I can look, right? A girl would have to be blind in one eye and unable to see out of the other not to notice how he fills out a pair of Levi jeans. I blush to myself and hand the brunette her frappe. For a few hours, I can push down the memories of last night, and enjoy my job and friends. My favorite song plays over the sound system, and I begin to sing along, and even dance a little behind the counter.

Caleb and I have always been like this. Our friendship is easy, fun, comfortable, and safe. Lately, I've gotten the impression things are beginning to change. We started flirting several weeks ago and it's nice. He's grown manly over the summer. I can tell he has been working out. He's a few inches taller, and his body is filling out nicely. He's very clean-cut, always caring about his appearance, but now he takes that to a whole new level. Freshly shaven, perfect hair, the braces came off, and WOW. Caleb became a hottie in a few short months.

I promised him one dance at the Homecoming dance. I wore an emerald green dress that matched our eyes. Our eye color is identical, which is both weird and unique. I told myself I bought that dress because it matches my eyes, not ours. I looked good in that dress. It didn't hurt that it fit me well in all the right places. I loved that dress. It gave me curves that weren't there. I secretly hoped Caleb noticed how the dress looked on me and liked what he saw. I felt magical in it. I had a feeling the Homecoming dance and that dress would change everything. It had. That dress is now ripped to shreds and tossed into the garbage. I never want to see it again.

It feels good to joke and laugh with Caleb for a brief second. I suppose the old me is buried deep inside somewhere. She's just surfaced, hasn't she? Or is that the last drop of the old me left? Everything has changed so quickly. In a matter of minutes, I became empty. I have nothing to give. There's nothing to offer now. *Broken.* The word echoes through my head constantly. Sadness sucks me in again. The rest of the afternoon drags on in a gray, murky cloud.

Four o'clock finally arrives, signaling the end of my shift. I made it through my first day after...well, after. Grabbing my purse from the back room, I head out the door. I just want to go home.

"Hey, Tomorrow, do you want a ride home?" Caleb asks as he walks out of the shop behind me. He seems a little nervous. "I'm going that way." He stutters a little but smiles, and I notice a muscle in his jaw pops.

"You live right beside me. Of course, you're going that way," I retort back and roll my eyes at him.

"See, even more convenient. So, what do you say?" He sounds almost hopeful. His behavior is out of the ordinary, even for Caleb. It's a little odd that he's offering me a ride. He rarely goes home after work; he usually heads to his friend Josh's house to play video games.

"Sure. Thanks." I head to his car. My feet are killing me, and I decide I might as well face the questions about Homecoming and get it out of the way. Caleb is good practice for establishing my story. The truth of last night will forever remain silent.

I love to ride in Caleb's car. He is the proud papa (his words exactly) of a shiny, midnight blue 1968 Ford Mustang. Better known as 'The Stang'. He and his father finished restoring it from top to bottom years ago. Definite labor of love. It took them the better part of twelve years to finish the restoration. Now, this car is his baby. I settle in the soft leather seat, and Caleb runs around the front and jumps in the driver's side. This car is his second skin. He knows it intimately. Turning the key, the engine purrs, and the radio booms. He had been jamming on his way to work that morning, and I hope he keeps the volume turned up. It's much too loud for conversation. We only have four blocks to our neighborhood, so maybe, just maybe, I can escape the questions a little bit longer. Caleb reaches over, turns the music down, and then turns it off. I groan inwardly. I guess I can't catch a break after all.

"What happened last night, Morrow?" He's direct, but I hear the sadness in his voice. "You never showed up at the dance. You didn't return my calls or my texts. If I hadn't seen your bedroom light on..." The memory flashes across his features; his knuckles turn white, grasping the steering wheel.

I clasp my hands in my lap to prevent them from shaking and say quietly, "I'm sorry, Caleb. I wasn't feeling well, so I came home instead of going to the dance." My stomach twists from the memory of running home from the school grounds. Somewhere in the nightmare, I lost my shoes, causing bruises and cuts on my feet from running barefoot. My feet are sore and aching from standing all day —a reminder with every step I take.

"You could have texted Tammi or me, you know? We looked for you all over the school." His tone is angry and fearful at the same time. "Tammi told us that she and

Jeremy dropped you off at the side door to the gymnasium. That's the last anyone saw of you, Tomorrow. Can you imagine what went through my mind?"

A cold chill runs down my body, and I squeeze my eyes tightly, trying not to remember.

"I'm so sorry, Caleb. My phone was dead. I got sick; it must have been something I ate at the game, so I went home." I try to sound convincing, leaving out the nightmare between getting out of the car and running home. "I forgot to charge my phone. It's still dead. I went straight to bed. I'm sorry I worried you guys." My voice cracks and trails off. I feel awful that I worried my friends. But honestly, I wasn't thinking of any of them last night.

Looking at him, my heart shatters. His voice tells me he's very hurt. "I would have driven you home. You should have come inside and found me if your phone was dead." His voice is almost a whisper. "I worry about you, Morrow. Don't ever do that again." That being said, he pulls out of the parking lot and heads for our neighborhood.

I remember seeing my best girlfriend as I climbed out of the back seat of Jeremy's car. Tammi looked stunning in her navy blue lace dress, which hugged her curves and accented her features. She has cascading blonde hair, a heart-shaped face, and sparkling blue eyes.

Tammi and her boyfriend Jeremy dropped me off at the dance. Jeremy forgot their tickets, so he and Tammi returned to his house to get them. I promised Tammi to go right in and find Caleb. I knew he was waiting for us and our other friends, Bree Phillips and Carly Goodlove. I didn't go right in, though. I wandered around the school, waiting for them to return. I didn't want to walk into the dance alone. I tried to text Caleb, but my phone was dead. The parking lot on that side of the gym looked pretty full, so I headed around to the back of the building, figuring they would park in the far lot, and I would catch them as they walked in. It was dark on that side; the floodlight was out. I didn't like being back there alone, so I turned around to return to the front of the building and ran right into *him*.

3

Today leans against the door jamb, watching me gather my books into my backpack. I take my time, prolonging the arrival to school as long as possible. I don't want to face Tammi, Carly, and Bree. I avoided their texts and calls all weekend. I knew Caleb would relay the excuse I gave him about why I didn't show up at the dance. I want to face them about as much as I want to face Today: the person *and* the time.

"What's wrong, Morrow Bear?" she asks, her brows wrinkled. "You're always the first one ready for school. You've been acting weird all weekend," she says in a motherly tone that tells me of her level of concern for my well-being."

"I'm just tired. I stayed up late finishing an English paper," I reply truthfully. Well, partially truthfully. I did finish an English paper last night but I completed it by nine o'clock. I tossed and turned in my bed like a tumbleweed the rest of the night. This morning, I feel like a truck has run over me, backed up, and run over me again.

"Okay, well, get moving. We have to pick up Troy," she says as she leaves my room, red hair swaying behind her.

"Wait, what? Why?" I call out, following her down the stairs. I feel my face flush as my heart rate kicks up a notch. I don't want to ride to school with them. No way. I don't care for Troy. He has a way of sucking up all the oxygen in a room. Troy is big, a wrestler, cocky (although Today describes it as confident), and assuming. He always makes me feel like a little mouse when he's around. Today is totally in love with him for reasons beyond me.

"His truck has a flat. Let's go," she urges, grabbing her keys from the hook by the kitchen door.

"Oh, uh, no. You go on. I'll catch a ride with Caleb. I, uh, forgot something in my room," I stammer, heading back towards the stairs. I move so fast that my feet get tangled in the rug, and I almost face-planted in the hallway. "I'll see you at school," I call over my shoulder.

I can feel Today's eyes on me. She knows something is going on, and knowing her the way I do, she won't stop until she figures it out. I can't let that happen.

I flash her my brightest smile and run back up the stairs, doing my best not to slam the bedroom door behind me. With my back against the door, I slide to the floor, pulling my knees to my chest, and wrap my arms around my legs, rocking back and forth. How am I going to make it through this day? I squeeze my eyes closed, forbidding the tears to come again. *Lord, give me strength*, I pray.

I listen as Today says goodbye to our mom, who's making coffee in the kitchen, and closes the front door behind her. I relax a little once I hear the car pull out of the driveway. Today and I usually ride to school together. We share a black Volkswagen Beetle that our parents gave us for our sixteenth birthday. Our older sister, Faith, drives a green Volkswagen bus she calls Pickle, so we also named our car. We named her Cricket because a belt chirped when we started her. I have my license, but Today thinks she's due the honor of driving since she's the older twin. Those eight minutes are monumental sometimes. She's good at pulling the 'I'm older' card. In retaliation, I've been known to pull the 'I'm the baby' card. Fair is fair.

Wiping my eyes, I collect my things from the floor and head downstairs. I'm not going to ask Caleb for a ride. I'll walk to school. It isn't that far. I know he wouldn't mind giving me a ride, but after our discussion on the way home Saturday, I think it best to keep my distance and let him cool off a bit. I'm going to have enough questions from my friends today. Mainly, Tammi.

Grabbing the doorknob, I hear my mom call from the kitchen. "Tomorrow, honey. Can you come in here for a minute before you go?" For a split second, I contemplate feigning not hearing her and heading out. I can't do that, though. It would bother me all day—stupid conscience.

"Yeah, Mom? What's up?" I ask casually, pretending to search the cupboard for something. Even though I haven't eaten breakfast, food isn't appealing anymore. With my head buried in the cupboard, I have an excuse not to look at her.

"I didn't see you much this weekend," she says. Mom works as a nurse at one of the hospitals in town. "And I wanted to touch base with you." She places her coffee cup on the table and sits down gracefully. I always thought she moved like liquid. Her hair flows like silk ribbons past her shoulders. Today and I get our looks from her; red hair, green eyes, and freckles. When we're out in public together, we are often mistaken for sisters. Our older sister Faith also has Mom's good genes. I'm glad Faith is away at school; she would nail me with questions, too. Mom is tall, toned, and elegant. I didn't inherit the elegant part. Today and Faith did, though. "Today said you didn't go to the dance on Friday. I thought you were going with Caleb."

I swallow the lump in my throat. "Yeah, I didn't make it to the dance. Something I ate at the game must have been bad and made me sick. I came home and went to bed." My rehearsed story comes out fluidly. I can't face Mom and lie, so I keep my back to her.

"How are you feeling now?" she asks with skepticism. It's hard to keep things from her, too.

"I'm fine," I lie. Oh, how I want to tell my mom everything and curl up in her lap like when I was four. She would understand. She would help me. There's no reason I don't tell her, except that I know she'll tell Today. There's no escaping it. It will have repercussions for her as well. Mom will be mad as hell and want to kill him. Her telling my sister is a given, and I can't let that happen. "All better." I turn and smile at her. My face feels plastic.

"Is there anything you want to talk about? Anything you want to tell me?" The love in her voice breaks my heart. She knows, just like Today, that something is wrong. I can't stand here any longer, or the whole story will flow out of me in one big, gushy mess.

"No, not really. I'm much better now." I inch toward the hallway leading to the front door. "I need to go though, I'll miss my ride. Love you." I wave and dash out the door. I start running as soon as my feet hit the sidewalk, and don't stop until I reach my locker.

Walking down the hall to my first period English class, I feel like everyone is staring at me. Am I sporting a scarlet letter or something? My cheeks begin to flame thinking about it. *It's your imagination*, I keep telling myself. *It's just your imagination.* I hurry to my seat at the back of the class, where Tammi and Carly are waiting for me with displeased looks. *Here it comes,* I think when I see them.

Tammi starts in on me before my butt even hits the seat. "What happened to you?" she snaps. "I thought you were dead!" Most of the class turns to stare at us after her outburst. Carly peers at me sadly, twirling a strand of hair around her finger, remaining silent. Tammi is clearly in control of this interrogation.

"I'm sorry, okay?" I stammer, my bottom lip quivering. "I got sick. I walked home. My phone died. Didn't Caleb tell you guys any of this?" I thought for sure he would have told the girls about my whereabouts.

"Yes, he told us, but I'm not buying it. You wouldn't have walked home alone. You would've waited for Jeremy and me to return to the school." Tammi is indignant. "Did you leave with someone? You should have told me. You scared us to death, Tomorrow Williams." She appears as if she might cry but is way too mad for tears. "What really happened?" she demands.

"Take your seats, everyone." Mr. Winters, our English teacher, walks in as the bell rings, and spares me any more questions from Tammi, at least for now. Tammi shoots me a fierce glance, telling me this discussion isn't over.

English is my favorite subject. Mr. Winters, a handsome, curly-headed man who happens to be my sister Faith's best friend's father, passes out the book we will read and discuss for the first half of the semester, *The Bell Jar* by Sylvia Plath. Reading through the syllabus on the first day of class, I was excited to see this book on our reading list. I've always wanted to read it. Now that it's assigned reading, I dread it. I no longer care to read the semi-autobiographical account of Sylvia Plath's descent into mental illness, ultimately leading to her suicide. What intrigues me the most about her is the work she could produce during such emotional distress in her personal life. Now I can relate, but I don't care.

The minutes click by slowly as Mr. Winters drones on and on, previewing *The Bell Jar,* and giving an overview of Sylvia Plath's life. I only catch snippets of what he's saying. "Born October 27th. Died 1963. London. *The Bell Jar. Ariel.* American poet." Having done my research early on, I already know all of this background information. I don't need to pay attention, so my mind wanders, and I doodle all over my notebook. It helps to pass the time.

When the bell rings, I'm startled out of a fog and shocked to see I have written *his* name all over the cover of my notebook in dark, black, jagged strokes. The script is angry. I've crossed out the name in many places. I have no memory of doing this. I shove the notebook in my bag and bolt toward the door, before either of my friends can stop me.

Running down the hallway, I ignore the shouts of hello from friends as I fly by. Colors blur together as tears sting my eyes. I'm an emotional wreck. I couldn't go a solid eight hours without crying all weekend, and I can't keep it together much longer. That's obvious. I can't eat. I can't sleep. When I do sleep, I have nightmares about him. Concentration has gone out the window. That was proven in English class.

I run faster, trying to get to the end of the hallway. I have to get out of the confines of the building. The gunmetal gray lockers are closing in on me. The smell of floor wax filling my nostrils is making me nauseous. The faster I run, the less progress I make. My feet are sluggish, like I'm running in quicksand, and it's swallowing me into its blackness. *Help me, God!* I scream in my head. Slamming through the double doors at the end of the hallway at full speed, I trip over my feet and am launched, headfirst, toward the steps leading to the first floor.

Strong arms grip me around the waist, pulling me back before I topple down the stairwell, and I scream, "No! No! Let me go!" Swinging wildly at the body that holds me, I'm out of control. "Stop! Let me go!" Over and over, I scream, terrified. "Help me, God help me!" Kicking and screaming, I try to get away. My heart thunders in my ears. I'm blinded by the fear of Friday night's memory.

"Tomorrow, it's okay," I hear through the mania. "Tomorrow, it's me, Caleb." His strong arms wrap around me, holding onto me. "Tomorrow, what's wrong?" He smoothes my hair. "Tomorrow, talk to me." He sounds as scared as I am but doesn't let go. "It's okay. I'm here. You're okay," he chants repeatedly until I calm in his arms.

Once I realize it's Caleb and not *him,* I cling to his chest, inhaling his scent. He smells like soap and citrus.

With tear-streaked cheeks, I peer into his eyes. "Please, Caleb, take me home," I beg, shaking in his arms.

Caleb nods and silently guides me to the parking lot.

4

"She has cheerleading practice," explains Tammi.

Since elementary school, we've been the Four Musketeers. It all started when Eric Foute threw sand in my face on the playground. Carly and Bree ran to me to help get the sand out of my hair, and Tammi punched him in the face. Eric cried to the teacher, but we all laughed. Tammi got sent to the principal's office and had to sit at the silent lunch table, our elementary school's version of solitary confinement, for an entire week. Right then and there, the bond was sealed. Sometimes, Today would hang out with us, but even back then, she had her own circle of friends.

"I just hope I passed." I wasn't confident about how I'd done on the test. I tried to study last night, but my mind kept drifting. I should have called Caleb to study with me, but I didn't want to bother him.

"Yeah, right. Like you've ever failed a test in your life, Ms. Brainiac." Tammi loves to call me that. It's true. I've carried a 4.0 throughout middle and high school thus far. Academics come easily to me. Tammi makes good grades but has to work hard for them. "The day you fail a test is the day the world ends," she proclaims, flipping her long blond hair over her shoulder.

"I'm going to get a chocolate shake. I'll be right back." Carly jumps up from the table and heads to the counter. She looks cute today in her white linen sundress and strappy gold sandals. Her black hair is short and charming, making her resemble a China doll. It fits her personality to a T.

"She has a crush on the blonde, built guy behind the counter. I think his name is Wesley Brooks," Tammi whispers a little too loudly. "She thinks she's being sly, but I know she thinks he's hot." I'm unsure if she means for hot-blonde-guy to hear, but Carly sure does. She turns and shoots Tammi a deadly look, but Tammi just laughs, totally unphased.

"So, what's up with you and Caleb?" Tammi asks, as she dips another fry in sweet and sour sauce. Now, it's my turn to shoot her a deadly gaze.

"What are you talking about?" I ask, turning to her. "Caleb and me? Nothing. You know we're only friends." I can't believe she suspects anything is going on. "Why would you even ask that?"

"I know he's given you several rides home from work recently, and he's always at your house every time I call," she says, as she quirks an eyebrow. "And he watches you all the time... in the cafeteria, during Student Council meetings, at Thanks A Latte." She counts off on her manicured fingers. "I've seen the way he stares at you." Tammi is always looking for possible hook-ups. She prides herself on spotting a budding romance before the couple is even aware. She's usually right, too, but not this time. Romance is the last thing I need right now. Besides, Caleb and I are very close friends. She knows that.

"Everybody looks at me during Student Council meetings. I'm the president. Besides, you know how Caleb is. He has taken on the 'big brother living next door' roll since he was ten." I roll my eyes for effect, but I know she's right, at least about the watching me part. Caleb has been more protective than usual since I told him what happened. He's always just a few steps behind me in case I need him, but he keeps his distance. I appreciate that he isn't smothering me. Other than asking me who hurt me at least once a week (which I never answer), he gives me space.

"Carly is shameless." I motion toward the counter, trying to change the subject. "Look at her batting those eyelashes like she's in a 1940s movie."

"It appears to be working," Tammi squeals. We erupt in giggles. Sometimes, we still act like elementary school kids. I've avoided spending too much time with them for the past couple of weeks, and apparently, they assume it's because of Caleb. You know what they say about assuming, though. It makes an ass of you and me.

Caleb texts me every night to check on me, but that's it. He understands I need time alone—time to think, heal, and come to terms with how my life has changed. I'm sure that's where Tammi's assumptions have stemmed from. She couldn't be more wrong.

Carly returned to the table, her cheeks flushed, and grinning from ear to ear. "Oh my God, he is so HOT! Finger-lickin' good," she says as she fans herself with her hand and melts into the seat. "I could eat him up. Did you see those dimples?"

"Uhm, Carly, you forgot your milkshake." Wesley, 'Mr. Hot Blonde Guy', grins as he sets her milkshake on the table. He must have heard Carly's comment because his cheeks are a lovely shade of pink. Lucky for Carly, he's standing behind her and can't see the shocked expression on her face or the red flames creeping up it. She got busted. As he walks away, Tammi and I dissolve into a fit of laughter.

"Shoot me now." Carly's embarrassment makes us laugh even harder. I haven't laughed like that in weeks. I missed my friends. I've spent so much time in my cloud of depression lately that, other than school, I haven't gone anywhere. By the time we leave Smashed Burgers, I've laughed so much that my ribs ache, but it feels good to laugh again.

We step out into the parking lot as the sun is setting. The sky has turned a dull gray, and I can smell rain. I didn't realize it had gotten so late. The last time I was out after dark was the night of Homecoming. My pulse quickens as tiny beads of sweat form on my forehead. I need to get home before the sun vanishes for the night. Memories flood my mind, and they are so real, like they are happening all over again.

"Tomorrow. What's wrong?" Tammi sounds alarmed. "You're white as a ghost." She wraps her arm around my shoulder, but I shrink back instantly. "What's wrong?" she asks again, clearly concerned.

"Nothing. I'm fine. I need to get home." I stammer and back away. "Will you take me home, Tammi? Please." I hate how my voice quivers. I shove my hands in my back pockets, so they won't see them shaking. "I really need to get home." It's getting darker now that the sun has gone down—every shadow leers at me.

"Sure, sweetie. Come on. Let's go." She heads toward her car, never taking her eyes off me. I fight the urge to run ahead of her, which will draw too much attention to the panic inside me. I walk across the parking lot with controlled steps, jump in the lovely silver Lexus her parents gave her as an early graduation present, and slam the door closed. Tammi slides into the driver's seat and turns toward me. I can feel her studying me, so I avoid looking her way. Instead, I fiddle with the seat belt, trying to fasten it, but my hands tremble, and Tammi sees them. Folding my hands in my lap, I wait for the barrage of questions I know she's about to sling my way. To my utter surprise, she starts the car and heads toward my house without saying a word.

The short drive into my neighborhood is silent except for the swooshing of the wipers across the windshield. The rain has begun and is coming down hard. I always loved the sound of rain hitting the rooftop. I love to sit in my bedroom window seat and watch the droplets hit my glass. Mom told us that when we were little girls, we complained that we couldn't go outside and play because of the rain. She told us it's God's way of giving the flowers and trees a drink of water. I found that thought comforting, and now I love rain showers.

Tammi pulls into my driveway behind my Volkswagen Cricket and parks the Lexus. I sit quietly, listening to the rain pelt the car's hood. The rhythmic tapping has a calming effect. My breathing returns to normal, and my hands have stopped shaking.

I know Tammi is waiting for an explanation about my behavior in the parking lot, but I don't know what to tell her. She deserves a reason for my freak-out session, but I'm not ready to discuss it yet.

"Do you remember that camping trip your parents took us on in the ninth grade?" Tammi reminisces. "The one where it rained all weekend, and we stayed in the tent instead of in the camper with your parents?" Her voice is soft, and I can tell she's lost in memory. Gazing through the front window, she continues, "You admitted to me that you had a crush on my brother, and I admitted to you that I broke your favorite music box, but blamed it on Today," she chuckles.

I nod and close my eyes. I remember that weekend well. The tent was damp, smelly, and humid, but we didn't care. We stayed in that tent the entire weekend; talking, laughing, and playing cards. We planned out our whole future on that trip. We decided to go to the same college, share a dorm room, and rent an apartment together after graduation. We planned our weddings down to the last detail. Tammi even knew how many rose petals her flower girl would drop. We discovered that we each wanted two kids; we would live side by side and raise our kids together. Of course, our husbands would be best friends, too. We had it all figured out.

Most importantly, though, we became blood sisters that weekend. I still have the scar on my thumb where we sliced them open to seal the bond. Tammi doesn't have a sister, so it means a lot to her that we're now blood sisters. Even though I have Today, it also means a lot to me. I have her back, and she has mine. Always. Thinking back, I realize we never told Bree or Carly our plans for the future, or the fact that we became blood sisters. We never asked them to become one, either. It's our secret alone.

Tammi turned slightly in her seat to face me. She held up her thumb to me, and I could see her scar reflecting from the lights on the dashboard. "I'm always here," she said barely above a whisper, turning back to face the steering wheel. I nod slowly, open the door, and run out into the rain.

5

Numbly, I follow Caleb up the stairs to my bedroom; he holds my hand the entire way through the house. Caleb has been in my house so many times over the years; he knows it as well as he knows his own. Once inside my room, I sit on the bed and stare, unseeing, at my desk across the room. The walls are painted "Purple Pizzazz," or at least that's what the color swatch from the paint store called it. This room has always made me happy when I walk in. It's my haven; somehow lively and vibrant, yet dark and cozy at the same time. I feel none of that now as I stare at the walls in my bedroom. I can't feel any of its former warmth. Even though the shaking has subsided, I am wrung out, worn out, and empty.

"Tomorrow?" he says, sitting beside me on my bed, tenderly holding my hand. "Please tell me what's wrong. I'm your best friend. You can tell me anything. Anything," he pleads softly. "You're safe with me." His words sound so sincere, and I believe him. I know I can trust him with the biggest secret of my life—a war battles inside me between confessing or holding it in. So far, keeping the secret hasn't worked out so well.

I turn to look at him, eyes red-rimmed and glassy. I feel the heavy burden I've been carrying fall away as I say it out loud for the first time, so even my ears can hear it. "The night of Homecoming." I swallow hard. "I was, uhm, sexually assaulted before the dance. I ran away and made it home." Sobs wrack my body as the words echo through my room and brain. I've spoken the awful, ugly truth for the first time. I cry for an eternity, eventually crying myself to sleep.

CALEB SITS on the edge of my bed, stroking my hair when my eyes open. I lie still, not wanting him to know I'm awake. Darkness spills in the windows, surrounding us like a heavy blanket. I must have been out for hours. The only illumination comes from a flickering candle night-light across the room. I study him in the soft glow dancing across his features for several minutes. His brow is crinkled, his left hand clenched in a tight fist, and his expression is fierce. He's lost in his thoughts and doesn't realize I'm no longer sleeping. I can almost see the anger oozing from his every pore. It's foolish of me to bring Caleb into my nightmare. I'm so selfish. That's what *he* told me. Maybe *he* is right. This isn't a burden Caleb needs to carry, and I wish I hadn't unloaded my troubles on him.

"Caleb," I whisper into the darkness. "I'm so sorry." I sit up and turn away from him; shame fills my soul. Part of me feels the relief of unburdening the load I've been carrying, but a more significant part feels guilty for laying this news on Caleb. Caleb is my best friend, but he doesn't deserve my pain. I can see he is shouldering it as well.

"Tomorrow," he says, alert at the sound of my voice. "You have nothing to be sorry for. Do you hear me? Nothing." He's very gentle, and his voice is tender. He sounds sincere, and for a moment, I almost believe him. But only for a moment. I know better. Sorrow wraps around me like a thick smoke, smothering me. He pulls me toward him, I assume to give me comfort and support, but I flinch at his touch, and he quickly releases his hold on me.

"Tell me what happened, Tomorrow. Who did this to you?" His voice trails off to a whisper. Caleb is, for the most part, soft-spoken, kindhearted, and easygoing, even though he's a karate expert. Everyone who knows Caleb loves him. He's what my dad calls 'a stand-up kind of guy.' He's stayed with me all afternoon and now into the late evening. He hasn't left me to wake up alone after my three word confession. I now fully understand what my dad meant.

Ignoring his questions, I ask, "What did you tell Mom and Today when they got home?" Panic starts to rise in my voice as I realize my family will ask why Caleb is here in my room so late in the evening. They will want some answers if they know I've come home sick. I jump up from my bed and pace, biting my nails, which are already down to the quick. What can I tell them to ward off suspicion? My mind races as I pace quicker between my bathroom and my bed.

"Morrow, sit down. Please," he pleads. "Nobody is home yet. Your mom left a note on the counter saying she's picking up an extra shift at the hospital and Today is at rehearsal with her drama team." Crossing over to the window, I glance out. The street glistens as its recently rained. I must have slept through it, which is a shame. I love the rain. When I was little, I would sit in my window seat, watch the rain pelt against the window, and imagine a tiny kingdom with a king and queen inside each raindrop. I wish I could escape into a raindrop right now.

"Talk to me," Caleb implores. His expression is grim as he pinches the bridge of his nose and lets out a slow breath. "Tell me what happened. Please." I can tell he's straining to keep his composure. Truth be told, so am I.

I sit down timidly in the window seat, clutching the stuffed Olaf snowman that Today had given me for Christmas last year. *Frozen* is our favorite movie, even if it's for kids. Today and I often dance through the house, singing songs from the soundtrack. Our favorite is "Let It Go," and I wish I was as brave as Elsa is in the movie. I can't face Caleb, so I speak to Olaf instead. He's heard the story before; Caleb hasn't. I have to be careful about how much information I give Caleb. I don't want him going off and confronting *him.*

"Tammi and Jeremy dropped me off at the door, but I didn't want to go in alone." My voice cracks as I speak. "I didn't want to go in by myself. I know it was stupid, but I didn't have a date..." I trailed off. Looking back on it now, it was stupid to care about walking into a dance alone. My friends wouldn't care. Besides, they knew I didn't have a date, and Caleb was waiting for me. It was his idea that we "go stag together." He said it would be the newest trend at our school, and he was pretty proud of himself for coming up with the idea. An idea that I had laughed at.

Caleb stays quiet, sitting on my bed, allowing me to go on at my own pace. "I walked to the back of the gym because I figured they would park in the lower lot since the upper lot was so full." I swallow hard, remembering how the events unfolded. "It was dark back there; the floodlights weren't on for some reason. You know how maintenance is at the school. Anyway, when I turned to go back to the front, he was right behind me."

"Who is 'he'?" Caleb demands, getting to his feet. I flinch back from him like an abused child. He sees my reaction, and sorrow bleeds across his face. "I'm so sorry, Morrow." Sitting back down, he clenches his fists until his knuckles turn white.

"He asked me if I wanted to sit in his car for a few minutes until Tammi returned. I said, 'Okay,' and then it...happened." I spill the last bit out so hurriedly that I'm not sure Caleb can understand me. I start shaking and crying again. The memory is so vivid. I shake my head violently, trying to erase the memory, but it won't disappear. Rocking back and forth, holding Olaf for dear life, the memories flood my brain, and I feel his hands touching me again. "He was so strong. I couldn't get away. I tried, Caleb. I tried. He wouldn't let me go!" I began working myself into a manic fit again. I repeatedly cried a mantra of "I tried! I tried", rocking harder and harder in my seat.

Caleb crosses the room in two long strides, sits beside me on the window seat, and takes my hands in his. I can tell he's shaking from anger. "Who is he, Morrow? You have to tell me," he says through clenched teeth. "Who is this bastard that did this to you?" I've never seen Caleb so angry in my life. "Who is this coward that raped you?"

"I can't tell you who it is. I'll never tell, but I got away before he...he almost ripped my dress off, and his hands were all over me. He didn't rape me, but he might as well have." I shake my head violently, remembering how his hands felt on me. "You have to promise you will never tell Today or my mom. Promise me, Caleb." I start screaming at him, frantically trying to make him agree to keep silent. "Promise me! You can never tell!" My throat is raw from crying for the past three days. My voice comes out jagged as I plead over and over with him.

Caleb wraps his strong arms around me, holding me firmly against his chest, and lets me sob into his shirt. "Shhh. It's okay, Morrow. It's okay. I promise." He rubs my back, smoothes my hair, and lets me cry until I am all cried out again. I know he'll keep my secret. Caleb is a stand-up kind of guy.

I don't know when Caleb left, but sometime before dawn, I wake to silence in my bedroom. The closet light is on, and the door is cracked open several inches. A stream of light shines across the white carpet, giving off a gentle glow. Apparently, Caleb didn't want me to wake up to total darkness. For that, I'm thankful. Too many shadows lurk in the darkness.

A sticky note on my cellphone says "I'm only a phone call away" and oddly, that brings me comfort. The alarm clock beside my bed reads 2:12 a.m., and I wonder if a text will wake him up. I don't think it will, so I send him a message. *Thank you* is all I can say, but it isn't enough by far. For now, it will have to do. I tuck the phone beneath my pillow, pull the covers over my head, cuddle Olaf, and drift back to sleep. Caleb is my rock, and I thank God for him.

6

"**H**ey, Morrow, do you want to go to the movies with us?" I glance up from the book I'm reading, *Pride and Prejudice,* and see my sister leaning against the door frame and quirking an eyebrow with interest. Maybe going out with Today and her friends will cheer me up.

"Yeah, maybe." I close my favorite novel and place it delicately on my window seat bench. I've read it so many times that the binding is coming loose. I keep meaning to get a new copy, but Caleb gave me this one for Christmas several years ago, and the thought of replacing it feels wrong. "Who's going?"

"Faith, Hunter, Troy, and me," she says, counting off the party members on her beautifully manicured fingers. "Oh, and I'm thinking about inviting Caleb." She winks not so innocently.

"Oh, uhm, no thanks. I want to finish this book," I stammer and pull the oversized shawl around my shoulders. I sink deeper into the window seat, diverting my eyes from Today's scrutinizing gaze.

"Come on, Morrow Bear. You've read that book a gazillion times," she whines. "Besides, Faith and Hunter are only here for the weekend, then headed back to school until Spring break."

Hanging my head until my chin touches my chest, I pick at a loose string on the hem of my sweatshirt. I want to spend time with our big sister, Faith, and her boyfriend, Hunter, but I don't want to go with Today and...*him*. I've avoided the brute for several weeks at school and even when he shows up at the house with Today, which hasn't been easy. He's always at our house. But the last thing I want is to be in a dark movie theater with him nearby.

"Thanks, but I think I'll pass."

"Okay, okay," Today says dramatically, which is her typical MO. "I won't invite Caleb."

I roll my eyes, throw a pillow at her, and chuckle slightly. The sensation feels odd in my soul. Has it been that long since I felt normal enough to laugh? The question bounces around in my headspace until the realization sends me back into my gray cloud. Somehow, the grayness enveloping me helps me feel safer. I am invisible, unapproachable, and out of *his* reach.

"It isn't Caleb, silly," I toss back at her. "How many times do I have to tell you we're just friends?"

"Whatever you say..." Today tosses over her shoulder and sashays out of my bedroom.

I sit in the window seat, hugging my knees to my chest, wondering why my life has changed so drastically in the past few weeks. I haven't done anything to deserve what happened to me. I'm the victim, not the villain. The rain starts to pelt against the window, and I trace the fat drops of water as they race down the glass. My life is like one of those drops sliding to the bottom of the windowpane.

Caleb is definitely cute. I remember Today's comment, and I can tell he is more into me than just a friend. Before the night of Homecoming, I might have considered our friendship moving to another level. But now, that's out of the question. Caleb knows the truth, and I'm damaged goods. My future is closed to relationships at almost eighteen years old.

Snuggling deeper into the shawl, I curl toward the glass and watch the rain fall. Before I know it, I'm fast asleep.

"Wake up, sleepyhead!" Caleb pounces on my window seat, jarring me from a dream and scaring me.

"What the heck!" I scramble to an upright position, pulling the covers up to my shoulders and tucking them under my chin. "You scared the crap out of me, Caleb!"

"Oh, gosh, Tomorrow, I'm so sorry." Remorse immediately clouds his expression. The startled look on my face clarifies that things aren't as they used to be with me, and he realizes it a little too late. Caleb steps away from me, chewing on a thumbnail. What happened to me is my nightmare, and he's paying the price as well. This isn't fair on so many levels.

"No, it's ok. I was sleeping and didn't hear you come in. It's okay." My smile is weak, but his facial expression softens, so I guess it's enough.

"So, what's this I hear about you not wanting to go to the movies with us? Do we smell or something?" he teases lightly. "I can take another shower if that's the problem." He has the cutest dimples when he reveals that mischievous smirk. Caleb is always the jokester. Some girl is going to be lucky to land him. Unexpectedly, the thought makes me sad.

Shaking it off, I stand and begin folding the blanket I had been snuggling under only moments earlier, with my back to Caleb. I don't want him to see my cheeks blushing.

Wow, my emotions are running from zero to sixty, and back again in a matter of nanoseconds.

"Funny," I say, turning away from him and explain, "I'm not up to a movie today. That's all."

"Okay, well, let's do something else. You need to get out of the house. Let's go to Bass Lake or Veteran's Park and feed the ducks." Caleb always comes up with the perfect ideas. An afternoon walking the trails at the lake might be exactly what I need to get out of the funk I've been in.

"Yeah, sure." I sound more enthusiastic than I feel, but the smile that spreads across Caleb's face is not lost on me. "Let's take Cricket." I love driving our black Volkswagen Beetle with its super dark tinted windows, but I rarely get the opportunity. Today always pulls the 'I'm older' card. She'll be with Boy Troy today, so I can use our car. The thought makes me smile.

"Whoo-hoo! Let's go to the lake!" Caleb jumps to his feet and rubs his palms together conspiratorially. The quirk in his eyebrow makes me laugh and feel nervous simultaneously.

"I know that look; it can't be good," I continue, raising an eyebrow. "What is that devious mind of yours planning?"

"I have a brilliant idea!"

"Yeah...?"

"While everybody is at the movies, let's soap the windows on Troy's Tacoma."

The vision of the last time I was in that truck sends shivers down my spine.

"Uhm, no. I'd rather not," I stammer and turn to stare out the window. My hands tremble as I pull the blanket under my chin again. I hope Caleb doesn't notice and starts asking questions again.

"Oh, come on, Tater. Last week, he covered the Stang in

sticky notes. Payback time!" He didn't see my reaction to the mention of Troy. For that, I'm relieved. I would love to pay him back for what he did to me, but that isn't going to happen.

"Boys and their muscle cars. But, how do you know it was Troy?"

"Because the sticky notes spelled out 'Troy was here,' and he's the only Troy I know. He's just lucky there was no damage to the new paint."

"Oh, well, I guess it was him," I stammer. "Let's just go to Bass Lake Park."

Caleb pouts a little but doesn't push the issue. He tosses me a hoodie hanging on my closet door and waits patiently as I pull my hair into a messy bun, and then pull the sweat-shirt over my head. "Okay, let's go."

BASS LAKE PARK is one of my favorite places in Holly Springs, especially in the late fall. The reflection of the brightly colored foliage and Carolina Blue sky off the water is stunning. Autumn in Holly Springs has a distinct smell, too. I take a deep breath and relish the aroma of fall as we walk through the trees to reach the lake's edge. The scent is hard to describe, but it's somewhere between musky and clean. I guess crisp is a better description? Caleb grabs the can of oats I snatched from the kitchen, and we head to the water's edge. Getting out of the house lifted my spirits a little, and before long, I was happy I had come. Caleb always knows what I need.

Caleb starts to drop little wads of oats behind him, leaving a trail to the water. It takes me a while to notice this; I'm too busy admiring the view of his backside. My face blushes when he turns to say something to me, catches me checking him out, and wiggles his butt at me. "Like what you see?" he chuckles. I can't believe he caught me.

"You wish!" I try to cover. "Are you trying to lure Hansel and Gretel to your gingerbread cottage?"

"Nope, I have my hopes set on something better," he winks and continues walking. I start to say something in response, although I'm unsure what to say, when I hear *honk! honk!* behind me. Several ducks have found Caleb's goodie trail, gobbling up the oats and heading right toward Caleb.

"See! It works every time."

It's stupid to think he was referring to me. He knows I'm damaged goods. My mood plummets again as I admit the fact to myself. *Ducks, he meant ducks.*

Sitting on a bench by the water, I close my eyes. The sun is warm on my face, as the waves gently lapping against the shoreline soothe my soul. The emotional rollercoaster has been on full tilt all day and it's exhausting. I have got to get ahold of myself, or I'll go crazy. I open my eyes and I see Caleb staring at me. At least ten ducks have gathered for their afternoon meal, and they are getting pretty loud, trying to get Caleb to toss more grains. I smile meekly, not wanting him to worry about me.

"Tater Bug, are you okay?" Concern is evident in his voice as he takes my hand and sits beside me on the bench. "You can talk to me about how you are feeling. You know that, right? I'm always here for you."

"I just wish he hadn't..." I trail off, not wanting to rehash the story again. He knows what happened but not from whom the attack came. "Never mind, I'm okay. I don't want to talk about it. Let's feed the ducks before they attack us." I fake a reassuring smile and grab some food from the bag.

He purses his lips and nods. "Okay, Morrow, whatever you want. Let's feed the ducks."

Caleb sits so close to me that I can feel his warmth through the fabric of my sweatshirt. I'm extremely cold-natured, and he's like my personal sunshine. He warms my body with his touch and my soul with his caring nature. For the millionth time over the past month and a half, I wish I was worthy of Caleb's affection. *He* ruined that for me.

"I spoke to my Aunt Kelly in Hickory the other day. She's a Stephen Minister at her church. She was telling me about the Stephen Ministry. They are lay people trained as Christian counselors to walk beside people going through a difficult time in life. The assigned minister has to keep all information confidential as a requirement to participate. Maybe it's an opportunity you might want to consider?" Caleb appears hopeful as he explains what a Stephen Minister is.

"You think I'm crazy now and need a shrink to deal with this?" My blood boils. He has some nerve, talking to his Aunt Kelly about me and what happened. Who does he think he is? I knew it was a mistake talking to him.

"What? Morrow, it isn't that at all. I didn't tell her the circumstances. I wouldn't do that." I stand, and he grabs my hand to stop me.

"Let go of me!" I yell at him and jerk my hand free of his. I've got to get out of here. I march off toward the parking lot and hear his pleas behind me.

"Tater, wait. I didn't mean to upset you. I'm sorry!"

I take off running and don't stop until I reach Cricket. Jerking the door open, I snag a fingernail on the handle, and the nail rips off. I'm so mad I don't feel the pain or notice that I'm bleeding. As Caleb approaches the driver's side, I slam the door closed and jam the lock. When the engine starts, I slam the car into drive and speed away, leaving Caleb standing in my wake. I refuse to look in my rearview mirror, fearing I might feel sorry for him and go back.

"Screw that," I scream at the windshield. "I'm not going back. I can't believe he thinks I need a shrink!" Cricket doesn't respond to my outburst. She's grown accustomed to my tantrums. "I think I'm doing pretty damn good considering what I've been through. Just once, I'd like to see how a guy would handle the situation if the roles were reversed." My huffing and puffing tirade continues until I reach my driveway. What a lousy day this turned out to be. For a split second, I worry about how Caleb will get home from the lake but decide that he can walk for all I care.

The house is quiet, which I'm thankful for. Everyone is still out. Once again, in the middle of the afternoon, I retreat to my bedroom, lock the door, and cry myself to sleep.

Knock, knock, knock. Gentle wrapping on my door wakes me well after dark. I can't believe I slept the day away. Groggily, I flip the bedside lamp on and sit up in bed.

"Who is it?" I ask in a stupor.

"It's Faith. I'm getting ready to head back to school. May I come in?" my older sister asks from the other side of the door.

"Sure." Sitting up, I pull my red locks into a messy bun. I feel an inquisition coming on, and I'm not looking forward to it.

"You okay, Half Pint?" Faith has called Today "Sweet Pea" and me "Half Pint" for as long as I can remember. I have more nicknames than anyone I know.

"I'm fine," I lie. It's good that my name isn't Pinocchio;

otherwise, my nose would reach across town by now. I've told so many lies since the incident that I'm losing track of who I told what.

"You've slept more this weekend than I've ever known you to sleep. Are you sick?"

"No, just tired. I've been staying up late with homework and stuff." I hate lying, but I have to protect Today and my secret.

"Hmm, okay..." Faith purses her lips. I can tell she isn't buying it. "How was your day out with Caleb? Didn't you two go to Bass Lake Park?"

"We did, for a little bit. Why?" Do I really want to know the answer to that question?

"Because Hunter and I saw him walking down Bass Lake Road after we left the theater." Her back is to me, so I can't read her expression, but I know she's fishing for information.

"I don't know. Maybe he was out for a run."

"Maybe. He was very quiet on the ride home," she says, her voice filled with skepticism.

Sitting beside me on the bed, she takes my hands in hers, and I wince. My finger is sore from losing the nail. I pull my hand from hers, but not before she notices the nail is gone and there's blood on my finger.

"Tomorrow, what happened?" she immediately grabs my hand to inspect it. "This looks terrible. What in the world did you do?"

"Oh, I slammed my finger in the car door." It isn't a lie, only not the whole truth. I can live with that. I hope she can, too, and not probe any further.

"Does this have something to do with why Caleb was walking home?" I can see the puzzle pieces falling into place in her head.

"No, not at all." I shake my head vehemently.

"I'm worried about you, Sis. You haven't been your normal, loving self this trip home. Is there anything you want to talk about?" Her words penetrate my heart. I can't speak for fear that the entire story will come tumbling out. I shake my head. "No."

When she wraps me in a sisterly, warm embrace, I can feel her concern. "I'm okay. I promise."

"You can talk to me about anything, you know that, right? I'm only a phone call or text away." I nod into her shoulder and fight to keep the tears at bay. "I'll come home from school anytime if you need to talk in person, or you can come up and stay with me, okay?"

"Okay, but I'm fine," I repeat the same lie I've told a hundred times. I only wish it were true. "You and Hunter should get on the road before dark." I fake a smile.

"Pickle is packed and ready to go." Faith stands and strides across the room. Before opening the door, she glances at me over her shoulder. "I love you, Half Pint," she whispers.

"I love you too, sis."

"I'm leaving Penelope here until after Christmas." Penelope is her descented pet skunk that we all adore. "You and Sweet Pea can fight over whose room she stays in at night. Don't forget to lock her cage." I left her cage unlocked *once* when Faith was in high school, and she ate a paper she had written. I swear I'll never live that one down. The memory made me smile.

With that, she's gone.

～

I MANAGED to avoid Caleb most of the day in school, which is a blessing. I'm not sure who is avoiding who the most. We have one class together at the end of the day, French II. Our teacher doesn't allow speaking to classmates, and definitely not in English. Unfortunately, I sit directly in front of Caleb, so eye contact is inevitable. I linger at my locker until right before the tardy bell and slip into my seat before our teacher takes attendance.

"Bonjour," Caleb whispers from behind. I don't respond other than to flip my index finger over my shoulder in salutation as Mrs. James calls the class to order.

"Désolé,' he says in a low breath that ruffles the hair tucked behind my ear. I'm surprised he's telling me that he's the one who's sorry, albeit in French, when I'm the one who left him at the lake to walk home.

When Mrs. James turns her back to the class, I drop a note over my shoulder and hear it land on his desk.

I THOUGHT you would still be mad at me for leaving you at the lake. I'm the one that needs to apologize, not you. I know you're just trying to help me. I'm so sorry and thank you. Will you please forgive me?
Tater Bug

HIS BIG, strong hand squeezes my shoulder, and a smile spreads across my face. All is forgiven; all is well. I'm more relieved than expected and my heart pings in my chest. This is a new sensation for me when I'm around Caleb and it's not at all unpleasant.

7

I push myself back from the dining room table that's loaded with food. The aromas of a huge prime rib and casseroles of every variety—from green bean to sweet potato—float through the air like clouds from heaven. I'm so thankful I decided to wear yoga pants for Christmas dinner instead of my skinny jeans. Right now, skinny jeans would be a nightmare around my belly. I am s-t-u-f-f-e-d! My mom makes the world's best sweet potato casserole, and her stuffing is to die for. She only makes it for Thanksgiving and Christmas, which is a treat. I undeniably have eaten more than my fair share today. But hey, it's Christmas, right?

Standing to stretch, hoping to move some food from my stomach to my feet, I sighed exaggeratedly. I'm feeling a semblance of happiness. My family and Caleb gathered for dinner, and Troy is out of town with his own family. For that, I'm grateful. I can enjoy the holiday without employing evasive maneuvers to steer clear of him constantly. When he's around, I feel like he's always staring at me, making me feel dirty all over again, so I escape to my room.

"Tomorrow Elizabeth Williams," my mom says, interrupting my food euphoria. "Where do you think you are going?"

"Nowhere," I yawn and stretch as the tryptophan hits me. "Just making room for dessert."

"Ohhh, I made a cranberry cheesecake," Faith touts proudly.

"Well, I made a delicious lemon meringue pie," Today tosses out.

"And I made the red velvet cake and pumpkin roll," Mom chimes in. You would think we're feeding a small village in the jungle with all the food and desserts made for only eight people. We'll be eating leftovers for days...not that I'm complaining.

"I have a great idea," Hunter says as he takes a break from shoveling the remaining Jell-O salad from his plate. "How about a competition for the best dessert? I'll be the official judge," he says as he rubs his protruding midsection and smiles broadly.

"What does the winner get?" I ask with a sneer, since I didn't contribute to the dessert table this year. I was on cooking duty, and that suited me just fine. Baking isn't my thing.

"Bragging rights for the year?" Today interjects.

"You're on!" Mom is ever the competitive one. "But I forewarn you, my pumpkin roll came out exceptionally well this year."

"I say the men judge the desserts after the womenfolk clear the table," Caleb says in a long southern drawl. Every female in the room shoots him a death look.

"Caleb should do the dishes by himself after that comment," I counter to a round of agreement from the members of the fairer sex.

"Okay, okay, okay," he says, heeding our warning and grabs a handful of dirty dishes from the dining room table. Laughter erupts and fills the space. It feels good to be with family and friends—laughing, joking, and enjoying the afternoon with loved ones.

"Wise move, my man," Dad winks at Caleb. "Men, let's all grab a load of dishes, take them to the kitchen, and let these ladies rest after all that delicious food they fixed. Then, it's game on!" He waggles his eyebrows and rubs his hands together, invoking another round of laughter from the table.

Once the guys have the dishes clear and the desserts placed side by side on the dining room table, the competition is about to begin. Mom carefully dishes out slices for each of the men. Dad gets the first plate of delectable treats; Hunter and Caleb are next. Mom is going by age. Poor Caleb —he's the baby of the male gender at this Christmas celebration.

"I think we should do secret ballots. I don't want to get into any more hot water tonight with the sweet, lovely, non-violent ladies that made these incredible desserts for tonight's festivities." Caleb lays on the sugar thick, presumably to make up for his earlier blunder.

"My my, aren't we lickin' boots tonight?" Today teases Caleb, turning his face crimson. He shrugs his shoulders and looks away.

"I think that's a good idea. " Mom rescues Caleb, as usual. She has a soft spot for him since his mom passed away when we were in elementary school. I'm not about to cut him any slack, though. I enjoy watching him squirm, maybe a bit too much, and giggle under my breath. "I'll get some paper and pens from the study."

The echo of her heels clip-clopping across the hardwood floors as she passes the front door in the foyer to Dad's study is oddly comforting. It's familiar and comfortable, like a thick sweatshirt and sweatpants on a chilly day. Mom wears scrubs all day at the hospital, so when she's home, she likes to wear less casual attire, especially on holidays. I look like a hobo in my oversized hoodie, yoga pants, and tennis shoes. Mom wears navy dress slacks and a white cashmere sweater, with her hair in a perfect bun. My mom is elegant, whether in work scrubs or her Sunday best, as we sit in our customary pew at church.

Mom assigns each dessert a number for voting purposes and passes out secret ballots to the guys. "Now, you need to rank each dessert from best to worst," she begins, "not that any of them will be bad, mind you, but list them in order of favorites. Fold the ballot and drop it in this little basket."

"This is so exciting," Faith squeals, clapping her hands together before looking pointedly at Hunter. "If you don't want to walk back to school, you better vote mine as best, buddy." Everyone in the room bursts out in laughter.

"I got your back, babe," Hunter winks at Faith. Even after being together for four-plus years, she still blushes at him. I think it's sweet and sickening at the same time. I glance at Caleb across the table and catch him staring at me. Tucking my hair behind my ear, I turn away, feeling my cheeks begin to burn. *Well, this is awkward*, I muse.

Bing bong, the doorbell chimes, breaking the tension between Caleb and me. "I'll get it!" I respond a little too swiftly. In my socked feet, I slide across the foyer, *Risky Business* style, and yank the door open.

"Well, hey there, hot stuff," Troy says, standing at the entrance with a smirk. "I haven't seen you in a while." He winks, making my stomach churn. I haven't been this close to him since that night at Homecoming.

"What are you doing here?" I question, stepping back from him. Cold chills run down my spine as goosebumps prickle my arms.

"You know," he ignores my question and whispers seductively. "You should replace that diamond stud in your nose with a flame." He touches me and makes a *hissing* sound. "You are hot." I feel bile rising in my throat, standing in his presence.

"Troy!" Today exclaims from the dining room when she sees her boyfriend in the doorway. She hugs him tightly, launching herself into his arms, and wrapping her legs around his waist. He winks at me over her shoulder, and my blood runs cold. How can he do this to my sister right behind her back?

"Hiya, babe. Dinner was a bore with the 'rents, so I came to spend the evening with you." He's all smiles and charm, and Today swallows it hook, line, and sinker.

"I'm not feeling well, Taddy. Tell Mom I'm going to lay down for a bit." Without waiting for a reply, I make a beeline for the stairs. I ascend the steps, two at a time, and run to the end of the hall, where I lock myself in my bedroom.

Sliding to the floor with my back against the door, I hug my knees to my chest. I had almost convinced myself that Homecoming night was a mistake, and he thought I was my sister. Now, I know better. Deep inside, I always knew that wasn't the case, but it had helped me cope with Troy's audacity to do such a despicable thing to me.

I hate him; I know it in my gut. It eats me up inside whenever Today talks about how wonderful he is, how she hopes to be Mrs. Whitaker one day, or how much she loves him. Part of me wants to blurt out the truth—that he's a lying, despicable, no-good son of a gun, and she can do better—but I don't. I keep it inside because I know the hurt it'll cause her. Still, she deserves so much better.

I honestly can't remember a time in my life that I hated someone. Other than Sandy Hall, for telling everyone in the fifth grade that I had a crush on Caleb. However, I don't think that counts as hate. I think it was merely embarrassing to get busted. Hate is a new emotion for me—I mean, genuine hate. I couldn't put my finger on the exact emotion I was experiencing until I was standing face-to-face with him tonight. I did what I typically do when faced with an uncomfortable situation. I ran. Instead of facing it head-on, I ran to the security of my room. But to be fair, it isn't like I was going to call him out for the harassment in the foyer with everyone within earshot. No, I ran to hide.

I slide my back down the closed door until my rump is on the floor and wrap my arms around my drawn knees. Tears flow freely as I let the emotion wash over me. Part of me is relieved that I can finally name what I feel for Troy; part of me is sickened with pain. I trusted Troy; I believed one day he would be part of the family as Today's husband. That all ended the night of the dance. I'll do everything I can to excommunicate him from the Williams family. I only have to find a way to do this without hurting my sister. That isn't going to be easy. But right there and then, on the floor of my bedroom, I vowed to make Troy Whitaker pay and not hurt my sister.

A plethora of plans runs through my mind in rapid succession. I keep hearing the song "Danger Zone" from *Top Gun* running through my head. I envision tampering with his brakes to cause an accident. No—I dismiss that idea because I don't want to kill him, and besides, I don't know anything about cars. I can poison his Jell-O, but again, no, the whole death thing. I can accuse him of cheating, but I would need proof. Oh, I know! It suddenly hit me. I can forge his name and sign him up for the military. Yeah, let them deal with him! That's a great idea, I reason, because Today won't be crushed. Knowing her, she'll be proud of him. Yeah, I think a kick in the boot camp is exactly what the doctor ordered.

A light tapping on my door drew me from my reverie back to the real world. As I pulled myself from the floor and crossed the room to the window seat, I said "Come in," to the intruder, who, to no surprise, is Caleb.

"Hey, Tater, are you okay?" Concern is evident in his tone. "You took off before the dessert tasting contest even began, and let me tell you, it was brutal!" He chuckled a little, and I saw a twinkle in his eye. When did Caleb get so cute?

"I think I overate," I lied. "My stomach wasn't feeling so well." I turned away from Caleb's stare, knowing he would see right through my facade. I never could lie to him.

"Mmhmm..." His eyebrow quirks, and I know I'm busted. "Are you sure it isn't the unexpected company that arrived?" Damn it, he noticed.

"I don't know what you're talking about, Caleb." I tucked a strand of red hair behind my ear. "What are you doing up here?" I needed to steer the subject away from Troy quickly before Caleb noticed the beads of sweat forming on my brow.

"Well, since you asked," Caleb says dramatically and plops beside me on the window seat. "I brought you your Christmas gift." His smile is broad and beautiful, and he has perfectly straight white teeth, and deep dimples. "I wanted to give it to you privately. Hunter and Faith always tease me about my lousy gifts." Is he blushing?

"Aww, you didn't have to get me a gift. You know that."

"Well, I wanted to make up for the ant farm I got you when we were ten," he winks.

"Yeah, they were fire ants!" I smack him on the shoulder. "I ended up in the ER and still have scars from the bites." That was a horrible experience, and I forbade him from buying any more gifts. Until now, he's abided by my banishment of everything wrapped.

"I promise, this gift is of the non-living variety," he declares as he hands me the gift. My laugh stops mid-chuckle when I spy the rectangular velvet black box.

"Caleb?" I question, not knowing how to properly accept a gift from a boy, even if he is my best friend.

"Come on, just open it."

"Uhm, okay." I trace the velvety top of the box with the tip of my index finger. Bubbles of excitement fill my insides, mixed with a bit of fear. I have no idea what's in the box, but I feel it might change our relationship forever. Taking a deep breath, I decide to face the future head-on, pry the lid open, and gasp.

"Oh, Caleb," I exclaim as tears fill my eyes and leak down my cheek. Inside the velvet jewelry box is a gold chain adorned with an amethyst stone and circular charm. The charm is engraved with "Tater Bug" in a beautiful script font. "It's beautiful."

"I'm glad you like it. I figured I owed you something nice after the whole fire ant thing." His genuine and sweet smile makes my heart melt a little.

Turning my back to him, I lift my long hair off my shoulders so he can clasp the chain around my neck. I shiver slightly as his fingers brush my skin. The sensation isn't unpleasant, although it is unexpected. Once the chain is in place, I let my hair cascade over my shoulder, but his fingers linger on my neck. I can feel his breath on my skin as he leans closer and whispers in my ear, "My Tater Bug." His lips gently caress the flesh below my left ear.

"Whoa, what's going on in here?" Troy bellows as he bursts through my door.

Caleb and I sit up straight, adjusting our shirts that aren't out of place, mind you, and mumble inaudibly "nothing" as I drop the charm beneath my Holly Springs High sweatshirt. In that instant, a thought flashes through my mind: *Have we been caught doing something wrong?* And then, *who is Troy to call us out on it?* My ire rises in an instant.

"Who do you think you are, Troy?" I demand. The hate I feel for him, the emotion I recently named, begins to fill my soul. A boldness overcomes me that is utterly foreign. "I'm not your little girl, Troy. That would be my sister. GET OUT OF MY ROOM!" My voice gets louder than I realize by the look on his face and the fact that I can hear my dad stomping up the stairs.

"What's all the yelling about?" he barks from the hallway outside my door.

"Nothing, Mr. Williams," Troy backpedals and becomes the image of a choirboy. "It was my fault. I startled Tomorrow when she opened the door and found me standing here, about to knock." He winks and turns to leave. "I apologize for scaring you, Morrow."

My dad buys his story as he pats Troy on the shoulder. Together, they descend the steps back to the main floor, joking about how skittish I can be. If only Dad knew the real Troy Whitaker, he would toss him out on his butt in a heartbeat.

"Morrow, is Troy the guy..." Caleb edges, his brow creasing as he chews on his thumbnail.

"Let's get back downstairs before Troy starts making up stories."

"Good idea," Caleb agrees. "I don't put anything past that guy."

I gently rub the front of my sweatshirt and feel the 'Tater Bug' charm and birthstone under the material. I smile as we walk back down to the family.

---

t 7 a.m. the following day, a text message on my iPhone reads:

TROY: *I saw you and your little boy-toy in your room and am not pleased. Just know, Tomorrow Williams, you belong to me.*

THE MESSAGE CONTINUES with a picture attached. The grainy photo is from Homecoming night, and any viewer can see my face (nose ring shining) with Troy kissing my neck—his hand on my breast. I don't remember him taking a photo. I thought the light flashes were lightning. The picture is misleading. It doesn't depict the terror in my heart, the disgust in my soul, or the chill in my bones.

A knock on my door shatters the silence of my bedroom and startles me to my core. I shriek, and my phone tumbles to the floor, screen up on the white carpet, as Tammi peeks around the door.

"Oh my gosh, Tomorrow, are you okay?" Her eyes bulge wide and her hand covers her heart. It appears that my shriek scared her as badly as it scared me. Stepping in, she closes the door behind her and spies the picture blaring from my cellphone screen. I hurry off the window seat and scoop it up, clutching it to my chest. By the look on her face, it's obvious she saw the picture.

"Morrow?" she asks cautiously, pointing toward my phone, "what is that?"

"Nothing," I blurt a little too quickly to be believable. "What are you doing here so early?" I know full well that trying to change the subject is futile. Tammi is a dog on a bone when she wants information—relentless.

"Oh my gosh, Tomorrow, you're shaking," she says, sitting beside me. Wrapping a protective arm around my shoulder, she asks, "What's going on?"

"Nothing. I'm fine, really."

"You're a horrible liar," she admonishes, taking the phone from me. Her expression changes from concern to questioning, and then anger as she reads the text, and studies the picture. "Troy sent this? This is from Homecoming, right? And that's you, not your sister. What happened? You said you got sick. I don't understand, Morrow." The questions come in rapid succession.

Unable to respond, reliving that horrible night, I hang my head in shame, rubbing my forehead. Without warning, the floodgates open wide, and the tears flow unchecked. Wracked with emotion, my shoulders shudder as the torrent of emotions flows from my soul. I'm tired of keeping this secret, but I have no choice. Tammi wraps me in a warm embrace, and I melt into her kindness. She strokes my hair and whispers, "Morrow, it's ok. Everything will be ok. I'm right here..."

Several moments elapse before I can pull from her embrace and sit back under my own power. I wipe my nose on my sleeve and sniff a few more times before the tears stop. Tammi handed me a tissue from the box on my nightstand.

"Thanks," I murmur.

"No problem," she says, inhaling slowly. "Now tell me the story behind this picture and what Troy means by 'you are his'?"

I didn't want to relive the entire incident, so I cut to the chase. "Troy offered to let me wait in his car for you and Jeremy to return. He attacked me, apparently took pictures before I punched him in the groin and escaped."

"You said you got sick," Tammi wrinkled her brow.

"I did." I retorted rather curtly. "I threw up in the shower after I got home."

"Oh my God, Tomorrow," she said, her face turning pale, "Did he...rape you?"

"Thank God, no," I can tell her sincerely. "Had I not incapacitated him, I don't know what would have happened." A shudder runs down my spine.

"I can't believe your sister is still dating him."

"She doesn't know, and you can't tell her." Clenching her hands in mine, I plead, "Promise me, Tammi, you won't say anything. Please, I'm begging you. You can't tell Today. You can't, it'll kill her."

"She needs to know what he did to you, Morrow. He's a jerk, yet she thinks the sun rises and sets at his command. He does, too." Anger rises in her voice.

"Shhhh. She'll hear you."

"She needs to know the truth, Morrow. She would want to know the truth."

"No. I can't. I won't." My lips purse as I stare into her

eyes, willing her to see I'm standing strong on my decision to protect my sister's heart. I'll suffer, so she doesn't have to.

"I think you're making a big mistake, but it's your decision. I promise I won't say anything."

Tammi hugs me again before I jump off the window seat and stare at the pictures covering most of the mirror above my desk. Some of my happiest memories are taped to that mirror. Pictures of summer vacations with my family: Today and I washing Cricket the day Mom and Dad gave us the car; Tammi, Bree, Carly, and I eating cotton candy after the hot air balloon show at Bass Lake; and my favorite picture of Caleb and I goofing off at Thanks A Latte, dressed as elves for the Happy Holly Days parade. I realize, sadly, that the girl in those photos—the fun, vibrant, happy girl with freckles and a bright smile—is no more. She's long gone.

"Tomorrow?" Tammi says softly, "Why did he send that picture to you? What does he want?"

The magnitude of Troy's text hits my gut like a lead ball. What did he mean by 'I am his'? Is he crazy? Did he not get the point when I punched him in his jingleberries that I wanted nothing to do with him? What does he want? The questions swirl in my head, but I have no answers—none for me and none for Tammi.

"Nothing," I proclaim with a confident and robust facade. "I'm going to ignore it. Knowing Troy, it's a joke. He's just teasing me."

"What kind of joke is that? I don't think it's funny at all." Tammi sounds doubtful, and I'm not sure she's buying my aloof act.

"Anyway," I say, clearing my throat, "What are you doing here so early?" The bedside clock reads 8:30 a.m.

"Carly is dog-sitting in Garner all weekend. I told her I would bring her a cappuccino from Thanks A Latte." She waggles her eyebrows. "Caleb is working this morning. Do you want to go?"

"Why would I want to go to the coffee shop on my day off?"

"Uhm, because Caleb is working. Duh..." The blush creeps up my cheeks, and she giggles.

"Hush, Tammi Jo, you know we're just friends."

"Mmmhmm, your cheeks tell me otherwise." Her bright blue eyes twinkle. "Come on, let's go."

I toss on a pair of jeans, a sweatshirt, boots, and I'm ready to go. My phone is in my back pocket, but I toss it on the bed at the last second. I don't need Troy's distraction if he decides to text me again. A day with my best friends is precisely what I need.

Tammi pulls onto Kentworth Drive and miraculously finds a parking spot right in front of Thanks A Latte. I spy Caleb's Mustang parked down the street. Butterflies awaken in my stomach. Pursing my lips, I will them to settle. It's only Caleb, after all.

"Hey, Morrow," Tammi turns to me before shutting off the engine. "Does Caleb know?" Swallowing the bile that instantly rises in my throat at the mention of the incident again, I tell her honestly, "He knows what happened, but not that it was Troy. You know Caleb, he would pull out his karate moves on Troy and kick his butt."

"Yeah, and he deserves it," Tammi retorts.

"Maybe so, but then Today will want to know *why* Caleb kicked Troy's butt."

"Good point. Let's go." She pushes her car door open against the whipping December wind, and I follow suit. It's time for some coffee!

⁓

A RUSH OF WARM AIR, and the aroma of brewing coffee and cinnamon buns embrace us as we enter the coffee shop. The familiar sounds of coffee cups clinking against saucers, the espresso maker hissing, the low murmur of customers chatting, and Caleb laughing behind the bar greet me as I enter my second home. Comfort washes over me like a warm blanket.

"Ladies and gentlemen, please welcome to our humble establishment, Tammi Brock, and our very own, Tomorrow Williams," Caleb announces from behind the counter and winks in our direction. The usual Saturday morning crowd erupts in applause, whistles, and catcalls. You would think we're celebrities with all the fanfare we're receiving. This crowd is used to Caleb's antics and usually goes along with his shenanigans. I see Vicki from the corner of my eye shaking her head. She has a smirk, and I know she's as entertained by Caleb as the rest of the customers. Half the customers show up on Saturday mornings just to see Caleb's live entertainment.

My face turns crimson, and I wish I had put on some foundation before leaving the house. Caleb knows I hate to be the center of attention. I should have known he would make me stand out, he usually does. Silly me for thinking today would be any different.

The crowd parts as we walk to the counter, like Moses parting the Red Sea. It's too early in the morning for all this attention, and I smack Caleb on the shoulder when we reach the bar.

"Ow," he pouts, rubbing his shoulder as if I've really hurt him. Of course, I didn't. I did, however, notice the firmness of his muscles under his T-shirt and blush at my realization.

Wait, what am I thinking? Not only is Caleb my best friend, but he knows what happened. He knows I'm flawed, broken, and damaged by my sister's boyfriend. Caleb would never want me. Not now, not ever. Without warning, I remember the feel of Troy's hand on my thigh, the other grabbing my breast and ripping my dress.

The memory is too vivid, too real. I can't breathe. My heart pounds violently in my ears, and I break out in a sweat. "I have to go," I shout, even though I'm inside, but I don't care. Panic fills my chest, and I turn and run to the storefront's glass door, knocking several patrons to the side while I'm in the process. A kaleidoscope of color blurs in my peripheral vision.

A cold blast of air hits me in the face as I burst through the front entrance. It feels good on my flaming skin. Inhaling large gasps of air, I calm my breathing and attempt to regain my composure. I must have looked like \a fool running out of Thanks A Latte, but I panicked. *God, what is wrong with me?* I ask heavenward. My friends must think I'm a basket case, and at this point, I do, too.

"Tomorrow, are you okay?" Caleb bursts through the front door of the coffee shop like a man on fire. His face is white as a sheet. Tammi follows close behind Caleb. She doesn't look much better than he does. I hate that I've involved them in my messed up life. They don't deserve this burden. It's mine to carry alone.

Raking my fingers through my hair, I assure them, "No, I'm fine. I just needed some air." From the look on their faces, I know they don't believe me. But what can I say? I've been a total basket case for weeks, and my emotions have a mind of their own. I hate what I've become.

"Air? Really? That's the best you can come up with?" Tammi shoots me her best 'get real' face, with her right hand on her hip and head cocked to the side. I've seen that look before.

"I just panicked, okay? What do you want me to say?" My defenses flare. I'm the victim here, yet I'm getting all the harassment. Dang, I had a moment of weakness. Am I not allowed?

"We're worried about you, Tater." Caleb's expression is grim and remorse washes over me. "You've been through a lot since—" he stops short, realizing what he's about to say.

"It's okay, Caleb," I admit, "She knows." I nod toward Tammi. These two are the dearest friends a girl could ask for. As if reading my thoughts, Tammi puts her arm around me and hugs me. She's the touchy-feely one, not me, but I allow her to comfort me. "But really, I'm okay, and you need to get back to work before Vicki makes you work a double shift for abandoning the bar."

He glances back inside the coffee shop, and a pensive expression splays across his features. "I just want to make sure you're okay," he says.

"He jumped *over* the counter!" Tammi gushes, and I catch the sideways glance Caleb gives her.

"Oh man, I'll bet Vicki freaked out over that. Really, though, I'm fine," I continue, smiling timidly. "I'm sorry I freaked out. I promise it won't happen again." I wonder if I can make such a promise.

"Okay, then. I'll head back in." Caleb hesitates. "I'll call you when I get off work," he says, disappearing behind the glass door.

"Did he really jump over the counter to come after me?"

"Girl, he was a man on a mission," Tammi coos, and we giggle. My friends always make me feel better.

"Hey, guys..." I hear a familiar voice behind us. "You two are out and about early." It's my sister, Today. Guess who's with her? *Troy*. Seeing them is the last thing I want now. "I figured you'd still be asleep, Morrow Bear." Today is the early bird. I'm more of a night owl. Rarely do I emerge from my slumber before 10 a.m. unless I absolutely have to. Today, on the other hand, gets up before the sun rises.

Troy pulls Today closer to his side and kisses her head. I don't miss the wink he gives me. My stomach turns as chills run down my spine. Tammi must have seen it, too, because she immediately came to the rescue. "We're headed to Garner to see Carly. Let's go Tomorrow, we're late."

"Oh, come on. Stay and have a coffee with us. I'm buying," Troy offers.

"Yeah, come on. It's like I never see you anymore, Morrow, and we live in the same house, for goodness' sake." Today argues. Her bottom lip protrudes in a pout. I've been avoiding Today for weeks, months even, but I can't be around her. I know what Troy is about, but she loves him. What am I to do? I hate him so much for coming between my sister and me. Today and I used to spend hours together, sharing about our days, our dreams, and our future plans. We were closer than just sisters, we were best friends. Twins have a special bond that's hard to explain. We can finish each other's sentences, sense when the other is upset, and even know when the other is thinking of them. Mom always says it's a twin thing that she'll never understand. All that's gone now, thanks to Troy. I can't be close to Today anymore.

"Thanks, but we need to get going. Carly is waiting on us." Tammi tugs on my arm, guiding me to her Lexus. "Maybe some other time," she calls over her shoulder but mumbles under her breath, "When hell freezes over."

"Oh, my goodness, of all the people to run into!" I exclaim as soon as I slam the door closed. "I hate him so much. What does he want from me, Tammi?" Tears cascade down my cheeks. "He has my sister. Why can't he leave me alone?"

"Now, don't get mad, but I have to ask…" she hedges, "Have you ever given him any indication that you liked him? Flirted a little? Anything like that?"

"NO!" Huffing, I slam my back into the seat. "Never!" I know I'm yelling, but I don't care.

"Okay, okay, I had to ask. I believe you."

"What am I gonna do, Tam?" I'm at a loss. I can't believe this nightmare. I had hoped this would all go away, but after that picture he sent this morning, I know that isn't going to happen. I'm trapped in his web. If I expose him, my sister's world will be shattered, and her heart will be broken. If I keep quiet, my life will be a living hell. I don't know what to do.

We ride silently for most of the twenty-five minute drive to Garner, each lost in our own thoughts. The barren landscape of early January whizzes by unnoticed. I hate winter. Everything looks dead. The trees, grass, and flowers are all hibernating for the season, and the scenery is bleak and dreary. Gray. Lifeless. Dismal. These words describe more than the terrain; they also describe me. I feel dead inside.

"Why don't you ask him?" Tammi breaks the silence within the car.

"What?"

"Why don't you ask him what he wants?" she repeats.

"Are you crazy? I don't want to speak to him."

"Well, ignoring him isn't working," she reasons. "He hasn't gone away; that picture and text prove that. I don't see where you have much of a choice. Ask him his deal, and then tell him to go rot in hell."

"I don't know, Tammi. I'm not very good at confrontation. You know that."

"Well, it's either you confront him, or he keeps harassing you. The choice is yours," she declares as we pull into the driveway of the house where Carly is dog-sitting. She is standing on the porch, wrapped in a blanket.

"Coffee has arrived!" she shouts over the rail.

"Oh, crap! We didn't bring her Irish mocha mint latte!" I abruptly realize. This day is just getting better and better.

"That's okay, guys. I have news more important than coffee," she squeals. "Get in here, I have to tell you something!" Her excitement takes us by surprise, and we look at each other, perplexed.

"More important than coffee?" I inquire, shrugging my shoulders.

"This must be good," Carly giggles, and we head up the steps to the front door.

Once we're settled on the sofa with two little poodle mix puppies vying for our attention, Carly inhales profoundly and begins. "Remember that hot blonde guy with the big muscles I was flirting with a few weeks ago at Smashed Burgers?" her cheeks turn crimson at the mere mention of said, hot blonde muscle guy.

"Yeah, what about him?"

"Well, as it turns out...he goes to the church I've been guest singing at for the past two weeks in Apex." Carly bounces in her seat, the excitement of her story exuding from her pores.

"And?" The anticipation is killing me.

"And...he came up to me the first time I sang and complimented me on my song. He seemed so shy, and OMG, I melted." Carly's grin spreads from ear to ear. Her excitement is contagious, and I smiled along with her and Tammi.

"Aww. That's so sweet!" Tammi clapped her hands together. "We gotta find a way for you to run into him again outside of church, though. An altar call isn't exactly a dating app." We all giggled at her joke, even though she spoke the truth. My dad always says, 'Behind every joke is a little bit of truth.'

"Wait!" Carly continued with her story. "This past Sunday, since it's my last week as guest vocalist, I got brave, gave him my phone number, and told him to text me sometime. AND THIS MORNING, HE DID!" Carly squealed like a little girl. I have to admit, Tammi and I did, too.

"What did he say?"

"His texts were adorable. He remembered me from that day after exams at Smashed Burgers. He doesn't work there, though. His aunt and uncle own the place, and he helps out sometimes. He was filling in for his cousin that day. That explains why we haven't seen him there since. Anyway, we texted for about an hour." Carly blushed as she recounted the text messages. It's cute to see, but it makes me envious. I want to live an everyday teenage life like my friends. Troy Whitaker took that away.

Carly's eyes sparkled as she continued talking about her texts with Wes for over half an hour. Tammi finally broke in, "Carly, breathe, girl. You're going to hyperventilate if you don't take a breath."

I had tuned her out about twenty minutes earlier, but Tammi's exclamation got my attention, making me snort-laugh through my nose. Granted, it's unladylike, but it broke me from my self-pity funk, allowing me to join back in their laughter.

An hour later, Tammi and I were headed back to Holly Springs. It was a good afternoon with my friends, and I'm thankful Tammi showed up in my room this morning. I had almost forgotten about Troy's text—almost.

As we head back toward my house, the memory resurfaces, and so do the questions. Why won't he leave me alone? What does he want from me? What am I going to do?

Suddenly, it hits me—I know how to deal with Troy Whittaker.

"I'm going to turn the tables back on him," I announce, breaking the silence as Tammi pulls into my driveway. We've been lost in our thoughts for most of the drive, and I think I startled Tammi with my declaration.

"What?" she exclaimed.

"I know how I'm going to deal with Troy," I sneer, and a rush of warmth runs through my body. "I'm going to beat him at his own game."

"And just how are you going to do that?" She raises an eyebrow.

"I'm going to turn the tables on him." Lowering my voice to a conspiratory level, I whisper, "I'm going to tell him that if he doesn't leave me alone, I'll show the picture to Today and tell her everything."

"Now, there's an idea I hadn't thought of."

"He knows by now that I haven't told her and probably won't." Giving voice to my theory builds my confidence. "The most effective way to defeat a bully is to stand up to them, right?"

"Right. After all, it can't hurt."

"I'll text him tonight after Today gets home. I don't want her around when he gets my text."

"Good idea."

I TOSS and turn in my bed until 3 a.m., trying to decide what to say to Troy. I want my text to be short, clear, and direct. I'm not very confrontational; I'm more of the peacekeeper type, but I have to stand up for myself this time.

I don't want to hurt my sister, and I won't if I can help it, but Troy can't have this hold over me. What does he mean, 'I am his'? Who does he think he is? And I thought he loved my sister. God knows she loves him with every fiber of her being. She's said as much on numerous occasions.

Grabbing my cell phone from my nightstand, I pound out a text:

Tomorrow: *Troy, if you don't leave me alone from here on out, I'll tell my sister EVERYTHING that happened that night. I'll also show her the picture you somehow took... ending your relationship with my sister forever. NOW, GO AWAY!*

I watched the text on my screen to see if he read the message. It only took a few seconds to get the notification that the text was opened.

After several minutes without a reply, I delete the text thread. It's finally over. I breathe a sigh of relief. I'm confident Troy will leave me in peace now. The butterflies in my stomach settle and I can finally sleep.

I awake at ten o'clock the following day to a beautiful blue sky outside my bedroom window. I slept like a rock and felt pretty good for the first time in months. Standing up to Troy did more good than I realized. My bedroom door flew open. Without knocking, Today barged in, startling me from my euphoria, marching across the white carpet with purpose.

"Hey, Taddy Da-" *Smack!* Her open hand slapped me across my cheek.

"Don't you ever talk to me or my boyfriend again! Do you hear me?" she spat in my face, enraged. I have never seen her so mad in my life.

"What are you talking about?" I managed to spit out, rubbing my stinging cheek.

"Troy told me all about how you tried to seduce him the night of Homecoming! Who do you think you are?" The blood vessels were popping in her neck. "He's *mine*, do you hear me? You'll never get your hands on him again. Forget we're sisters. As a matter of fact, forget you even know me. I'll *never* speak to you again!" With that, she whirled on her heel. She was gone, leaving me in a state of shock. Troy turned everything around on me, and my sister bought it. How can this be happening? Today's handprint hurts my cheek, but not nearly as badly as my heart.

9

It's early morning on January third—our eighteenth birthday. Today hasn't spoken to me in three days and my heart is broken. We've never gone twenty-four hours without speaking since birth, so this is uncharted territory. She leaves the house early and returns late in the evenings to avoid seeing me.

Our parents haven't noticed that we aren't interacting with each other; if they have, they haven't mentioned it. My Dad always said, 'They'll work it out themselves.' And we always have. This time, I'm not so sure. I can tell her the truth, but if she believes me, it'll kill her. Since Troy made up his version and got to Today first, I doubt she'll listen to me anyway.

Sighing, I drag my butt out of bed and grab my fluffy purple robe from the hook behind the bathroom door. Definitely not looking stylish in my fuzzy pink slippers, I pull my long red locks into a ponytail and trudge downstairs for a much-needed coffee. It's way too early to be up and about, but I can't sleep any longer. It's only 8 a.m., and the sun has barely risen. See, it is too early to be up.

I hear voices rising from the kitchen and quicken my pace down the stairs. Normally, we have chocolate chip pancakes covered in whipped cream for our birthday breakfast. I hope this year is the same. Rounding the corner from the dining room, I spy Mom, Dad, and Caleb huddled around the kitchen island, but no Today.

"Caleb?" Everybody jumps at the sound of my unexpected voice. "What are you doing here so early?"

"Tater!" He doesn't miss a beat and says, "Happy Birthday!" He launches from the stool to wrap me in a big birthday hug.

"Uhm, thanks," I mumble, self-conscious of how I look. I'm pretty sure I have raccoon eyes from the mascara I didn't remove before going to bed, and quite possibly, some dried drool crusted in the corners of my mouth. I don't miss the fact that he didn't answer my question.

"Isn't it a little early for you to be in my kitchen?" I ask wearily.

"Heck no, I wanted to be the first to wish you a happy birthday." He pulls off the innocent act so well, but I know better. Caleb sleeps later than I do unless we have to be at school or work. I'm not buying the birthday excuse.

"Happy Birthday, sweetheart!" Mom embraces me in a heartfelt hug, breaking the tension between Caleb and I.

"You're up early, Half Pint." Dad joins the embrace. "Happy eighteenth birthday." I feel like we're re-enacting an episode of *The Waltons*. "My little girls are adults now." Dad's eyes mist over, and Mom dabs hers with a tissue.

"Mom, Dad, let's not get all emotional. I haven't had coffee yet. Save the tears for when I am sufficiently caffeinated." I'm only half joking. It's way too early for so much emotion from my parents.

"Oh, you're such a sour puss," Caleb chimes in rudely,

although I'm grateful for the levity he brings to the situation. I shoot him a mocking look as I head for the coffee pot. I can always count on Mom for a fresh pot of joe brewing.

"Where's Today?" Mom glances at her watch and creases form on her forehead. "I have to be at the hospital in an hour."

"She isn't here?" I'm a little shocked, but only a little.

"No, she said she and Troy have something to take care of this morning." I can hear the disapproval in her tone as she starts mixing chocolate chips into the pancake batter in a large, yellow mixing bowl. "If she doesn't hurry, she'll have to make her own pancakes."

"I'll eat her share," Caleb interjects, but nobody laughs.

"She knows this is how we start our birthday," I pout, but in my heart, I know she's avoiding me and our birthday tradition. Taking a long sip of my coffee, feeling somewhat human again, I try to reassure my mom. "Don't worry, Mom, Caleb will eat her share. Toss those bad boys on the griddle."

"Let the feast begin!" Dad is ready to chow down and so am I.

Thirty minutes later, with full stomachs and sticky fingers, Today finally waltzed through the back door.

"Nice of you to join us." Sarcasm drips from Mom's lips.

"Sorry, Troy and I had an appointment to keep this morning," she says, but she doesn't sound sorry. Her tone is flippant and dismissive.

"Well," Mom reacts, matching Today's tone, "Are you going to make it for dinner tonight at least?"

"Oh, yes, I wouldn't miss tonight's dinner for the world." Today sounded a bit too eager for dinner, in my opinion, but what do I know?

"I have to go to the hospital. I'll be home by four." Mom

kisses Dad as she grabs her car keys from the hook by the back door. "You'll have to make your own pancakes."

"Troy took me to Eggs Up Grill for breakfast, so no pancakes for me."

"But chocolate chip pancakes for our birthday breakfast have been our tradition since we were five." My mouth gapes open and I stare at her in disbelief.

Flipping her hair over her shoulder with a sneer, she replies flatly, "Things change," and leaves the kitchen without another glance, as we pick our jaws up off the floor.

Mom has tears in her eyes, and Dad slams his newspaper down on the countertop. I feel nauseous and Caleb voices what we all seem to be thinking; "What was that?"

THREE HOURS LATER, I still sit in my pajamas on my bed. This morning's shock is slowly disappearing, yet I still can't believe Today blew off our breakfast. Today said she was coming to dinner tonight. At least she's keeping that tradition. We always go to Osha Thai Kitchen & Sushi for special occasions, so the fact that she's still going makes me feel a little better. Still, we've never spent our birthday apart, and I haven't seen her at all today. She took off in Cricket right after Mom left for the hospital and hasn't returned yet.

My heart hurts because of the wedge Troy created between my sister and me. I hate him so much. First, the assault, then the text, followed by the lie he told Today... when is it going to end? *How* is it going to end? The questions keep circling in my head. Sighing deeply, I take my iPhone from my purse and text Caleb.

Tomorrow: *This has been the most depressing birthday in history.*

Caleb: *I'm sorry, Tater Bug. Today still isn't speaking?*

Tomorrow: *She isn't even here. She left a few hours ago.*

Caleb: *Where did she go?*

Tomorrow: *Who knows? Probably somewhere with Troy or her dance team. She never said a word...she just left.*

Caleb: *Wow, she's something else. Hey, wanna get out of the house and do something?*

Tomorrow: *Sure. That sounds good. We aren't meeting Faith at Osha until 5:00, so I have a few hours free.*

Caleb: *Awesome. Whatcha wanna do?*

Tomorrow: *I dunno know. You pick.*

Caleb: *Let's grab a coffee at Thanks A Latte.*

Tomorrow: *On your day off? Are you sure you want to go there?*

Caleb: *You got it. Anything for you, Birthday Girl. Meet me at the Stang in thirty. K?*

Tomorrow: *K*

∼

AN HOUR LATER, Caleb and I are nestled at a table in the corner. I sit with my back to the door because Caleb has this irrational fear of not being able to see who is coming in at all times. You would think we live in Chicago or Detroit, not peaceful, tiny Holly Springs, North Carolina; where the streets roll up at 9:00 p.m.

"I'm sorry your birthday has been so crappy, Tater."

"I can't believe Today won't talk to me. At all." Methodically swirling the foam on my double white chocolate latte with a swizzle stick, I recount the morning's events in my mind. "She ditched our birthday breakfast and spent the entire morning...God only knows where, and this is all because..." I trail off, remembering that Caleb doesn't know about the text from Troy or the lie he told Today. Now, I'm in a real pickle because I know Caleb won't let the "because…" go without an explanation.

"Because what?" His eyebrows wrinkled. "Did you two have a falling out over who got to eat the Fred Flintstone vitamin and who got to eat Barney this morning?"

I want to be mad at him for such a ridiculous reason for Today and me not to be speaking, but in reality, we've had that argument in the past. I'm also relieved that I didn't have to come up with a lie. I'm a horrible liar and he knows it. He can ALWAYS tell when I am lying.

"Yeah, something like that," I mumble and quickly sip my coffee.

"Always pick Barney, and she can't complain." Caleb has such a simple view of life. He's probably better off for it.

I hear the chime of the bell hanging on the door, alerting the staff that a customer is coming in. After working here for so long, that bell is programmed to grab my attention. From behind my back, I hear the faint humming of a familiar song. I cock my head like a puppy listening for his momma, trying to decipher the song. Then it hits me. Someone is humming "Happy Birthday." This can't be a coincidence.

Turning in my seat, I see a band of misfits—Tammi, Jeremy, Carly, Wesley, Bree, and some random girl I don't know—approaching our table carrying helium balloons, a cake with lit candles, and wearing party hats. The group bursts into full-blown song, and Thanks A Latte patrons join in the impromptu flash mob of "Happy Birthday". My heart swells in my chest as my face turns blood red. I have the craziest friends!

"Oh my gosh!" I jump from my seat, grabbing my friends in a warm embrace. "What are you guys doing here?"

"We heard a birthday girl was in the coffee shop, so the birthday brigade had to investigate!" Tammi is all smiles as she spins the tale.

"Oh, really?" I eyeball Caleb, knowing full well he's behind this little surprise, and I love him for it. He always knows exactly what I need.

Someone behind the counter brings a stack of plates, forks, and napkins for the celebration. Grabbing chairs and scooting two tables together, my friends gather around me, leaning in for hugs and a few cheek kisses. I'm overcome with love and emotion, which isn't my style. But I must admit, it feels pretty darn good right now.

"Blow out the candles and make a wish," Caleb instructs and winks at me. "If you wish for a handsome, debonair date for this weekend, I'm available."

Rolling my eyes, I feel my ears burn. Am I blushing? Oh goodness, now I'm very embarrassed and feel Tammi's eyes on me. She's determined to make a love connection between Caleb and me.

"You guys are the best," I gush with emotion. "I *so* needed this today. But how did you know we were here?" I ask, already suspicious of the answer.

"Caleb sent out the bat signal that you needed a special birthday surprise," Bree volunteers, beaming from ear to ear.

"I'm Ashlynn Brooks, by the way. I'm Wesley's sister." She extends a manicured hand as a way of greeting. She's gorgeous. Her hair is long and blonde, highlighted to perfection with a runway-worthy smile. "My brother sucks at introductions. Happy birthday, Tomorrow."

"It's so nice to meet you. Thank you for coming." I shake her hand awkwardly. Ashlynn sounds so sweet, and I like her on the spot. "I haven't seen you at school. Do you attend UNC?"

"No, I lived in California with my dad up until Christmas. He got remarried a few months ago, and I couldn't deal with the step-monster." The face she made, mimicking her stepmother, makes us all laugh. "So, I moved back in with my mom. I'll be starting Holly Springs High next week when the semester begins. I'm a senior."

"Awesome!" Carly chimes in. "We're all seniors, too. We'll show you around school, and you can hang out with us." I can tell she's eager to impress Wes, but Ashlynn seems like a doll. I think she'll fit in well with our group.

"You guys!" Looking each one in the eye, I let my emotions hang on my sleeve. "This is the perfect surprise. This day started as a pretty crappy eighteenth birthday, but thanks to all of my old and new friends, this has turned out to be quite memorable. Thank you all so much." Wiping a tear from my eye, I turn to Caleb and continue. "Caleb Logan, what would I do without you? Thank you for always coming to my rescue," I say sincerely and kiss him on the cheek.

In typical Caleb fashion, he plasters a hand over his cheek and pretends to faint. "I shall never wash this cheek again."

"You are such a ham."

∼

OSHA ISN'T CROWDED when we arrive for our reservation. "Osha" means tasty in Thai, and the restaurant lives up to the name. Mom orders their signature Thai Town Mule to sip before dinner, and I order a Diet Coke. Dad has his customary sweet tea. I don't know how he drinks tea but to each his own.

"Happy Birthday!" Faith waltzes towards our table, in her typical exuberant fashion. I love my oldest sister to death. She's like a breath of fresh air, filling the room with joy. I'm so happy she made it in from school for our birthday dinner. She'd visited for Christmas but returned to school and Hunter the day after.

"You made it!" I jump up and hug her fiercely. After the alienation from Today, I need to be in Faith's warm embrace.

"Of course, I made it, Half Pint. I wouldn't miss your eighteenth birthday for anything in the world." She releases me from her hug and kisses me lightly on my forehead. "Hunter is bummed that he couldn't come but understands that birthday dinners are for family only. No boyfriends allowed."

"Well, that's the rule," Dad reiterates Faith's statement, giving his oldest a fatherly hug and kiss.

"Tell him we miss him but appreciate his understanding." Mom loves on her daughter before returning to her seat and cocktail.

"Where's Today?"

"She should be here soon," I inform Faith, hoping Today keeps her word from this morning.

"So, how has your big day been so far?" Faith says as she turns to me. I fill her in on the details of the impromptu party at Thanks A Latte that Caleb arranged.

"That boy loves you. You should put him out of his misery and go out with him." I don't miss the wink she gives me.

"Why does everybody say th-"

"Hi!!" Today announces as she and Troy burst through the entrance of Osha. What's he doing here? Hunter respected that birthday dinners are for family only. What makes Troy think he's so special that he can intrude on our family's tradition?

"Umh, hi guys." Dad stands up on his feet—six feet, six inches of dad-ness. "This is a family dinner. I don't mean to be rude, Troy, but Today knows no boyfriends are allowed."

You go, Dad! I think. Neither Troy nor Today shrinks back after Dad's declaration. What's going on here? Today has pulled some stunts in her time, but this one is over the top. Troy needs to go.

"Well, you are correct, Daddy." Today smiles and snuggles up to Troy, making me sick. "Boyfriends aren't allowed at birthday family dinners, but tonight is different. Troy gave me the ultimate birthday gift."

After a moment of silence, nobody asked what the gift might be. Today extends her left hand, weighed down with a sizable diamond on her ring finger. "Troy and I got married this morning!"

10

"You *what*?" Dad explodes. His chair scrapes the tile and skids backward as he stands, sending chills up my spine. It's worse than nails on a chalkboard. Veins and muscles bulge in his neck and forehead, which I've never seen before. Mom gulps the remainder of her cocktail, Faith gasps, and I sit dumbfounded in my seat. This is NOT how I expected our eighteenth birthday to turn out.

"Calm down, Daddy," Today purrs, unphased by Dad's reaction to her news. She wraps an arm around Troy's waist. "It isn't like we weren't going to get married someday anyway. We just made it happen sooner rather than later." She snuggles closer to Troy, and he smirks. *Arrogant bastard,* is all I can think. Also, that I'm going to be sick.

"Don't tell me to calm down, Today Elizabeth," Dad's voice booms throughout the restaurant. I'm thankful that it's still early and only a few patrons are in the restaurant. Still, every eye is on our table. I can only shake my head slowly in disbelief. How could she do this? "I forbid you to get married. You haven't even graduated high school."

"Richard—," Troy speaks up for the first time since their arrival.

"That's 'Mr. Williams' to you, and I would advise you to leave, young man. I'm not afraid of going to jail." Wow, Dad isn't playing. My head is on a swivel as the conversation bounces from person to person. I can't believe this is happening. I feel trapped in a bad episode of *The Twilight Zone*.

"Dear, you are making a scene," Mom says as she touches Dad's arm tentatively, quickly glancing around the restaurant. I notice the staff has stopped to watch the drama unfolding. The scene is beyond embarrassing.

"You're damn right I'm making a scene." Dad's bellow reverberates off the glass windows. "No daughter of mine is getting married at eighteen!"

"How about we take this conversation back to the house?" Faith offers, pushing back from the table. "Before someone calls the cops."

"I think that's a good idea," Mom concurs. Dad doesn't look convinced but doesn't protest.

"Drinks on the house," the owner shouts from behind the counter. I think he wants us out of his establishment as soon as possible. I don't blame him one bit. "Just go."

THE RIDE HOME from the restaurant is beyond tense. Dad's knuckles are white as he grips the steering wheel, and the muscles in his back are tight. He's coiled tighter than a cobra, ready to strike a rat. And that rat's name is Troy Whitaker. Mom is sitting in the passenger seat, sniffling into a Kleenex. I'm huddled in the back seat of Mom's Escalade, followed by Faith in her VW Bus, Pickle.

How can Today disrupt our happy little family this way? And what's up with Troy? I don't get it. Why did he send me that text saying he would make me his (granted, I don't want him) and then marry Today? Even though I know she'll never believe me over her 'husband,' maybe their marriage will benefit me. Hopefully, now, Troy will leave me alone, and I'll find some peace. Time will tell.

Pulling into the garage, I pray, asking God to be in the center of the horrible conversation I know will occur once Today and Troy arrive.

God, please help my family during this difficult time. Please keep tempers calm, bring peace to the conversations, and keep my dad from punching Troy in the face. Amen.

"I need a scotch," Dad announces as he leaves the confines of the car. If I were old enough, I would ask to join him.

"Yes, a drink to calm our nerves might help," Mom agrees, apparently forgetting she had a Thai Town Mule at the restaurant. They disappear into the house.

"Did you have any idea they would pull a stunt like this?" Faith asks as she slides onto the leather seat beside me. "I can't believe Today did this...married on her eighteenth birthday! She has her whole life ahead of her. I'm glad Hunter and I decided to wait until after college to get married."

"Well, to be fair, Faith, you two share an apartment. Mom and Dad would freak out if they knew that. I think they would rather you two got married."

"Shhh...not so loud. They might hear you."

"Pfft, they are already in Dad's study raiding the liquor cabinet," I counter. "But still, I think you should eventually tell them."

"But not tonight!" We say in unison and somehow find it

within us to giggle in the middle of this disaster. We sit in silence, mulling over what has and will happen, and then Faith leans over and hugs me. We sit cuddled in the back seat until the overhead garage door light clicks off, and we're surrounded by blackness. I can't help but feel that the dark garage has been a metaphor for my life since Homecoming. *Can the blackness get any darker*, I wonder. I think the Williams family is about to find out.

Faith turns on her cell phone's flashlight feature, and we sit silently, staring at the glow. When we hear the rumble of Troy's truck pulling into the driveway, Faith sighs deeply. "Well, here we go," she murmurs. "Let the games begin."

"IT'S BEEN TWO HOURS," Faith whines into Penelope's black-and-white fur. "I want to know what's going on down there and, more importantly, cut into that amazing Oreo cake from Asia's Cakes and Company in the fridge. Have you seen it?"

"No, I haven't. They got us a cake from Asia's? Oh my gosh, they are the most amazing cakes ever!"

"Yup! I saw it when I got some strawberries for Penelope from the fridge," she says, licking her lips. "One side is the moon for Today, and the other is the sun for you. Mom's so clever to think of that theme. They went all out for your eighteenth birthday."

"Yeah, and Today ruined it," I say. Knowing we won't share that cake this year, my heart sinks a little. I hate Troy for what he's done to this family.

"Hey, Faith, there's something I haven't told you..."

I'm ready to spill my guts about Homecoming to my big sister. I don't see how things can get any worse.

"Okay, what's up, Sweet Pea?"

"Well, remember you asked me over Thanksgiving break if something was wrong?" I begin.

"Yeah, I remember."

"Well, what I didn't tell you was—"

Troy's truck comes to life in the driveway without warning, breaking the momentum of my confession.

"They're leaving!" Faith exclaims, jumping from my bed. She rushes across the room and places Penelope back in her crate, and the skunk squeaks in displeasure. "Let's go."

Upon reaching the landing at the top of the stairs, I see Today marching toward us. Her face is scrunched, obviously unhappy. Looking up, she glares at me like the time I stole her lollipop and threw it in the dirt. "You'll never get him now," she sneers in my direction, knocking me aside with her shoulder and slamming her bedroom door behind her.

"What was that all about?" Faith questions, eyebrows furrowed.

I shrug my shoulders and quirk one side of my mouth upward. "Who knows?" I do know, but that doesn't make her actions any clearer in my mind. All I know is she married a loser.

The scene in Dad's study splinters my heart. Mom is in an oversized leather chair, crying, while Dad sits behind his desk, nursing a scotch. Neither one looks up as Faith and I enter the room. Several moments of awkward silence pass before Faith's voice shatters the silence. In her typical, outgoing, over-the-top way, she asks the question on both our minds, "Well?"

Dad sighs hard and closes his eyes. "The marriage is legal. There's nothing we can do." Mom sniffs from her chair. "For the life of me, I don't know why Today did this."

"What did we do so wrong?" Mom asks, sounding

brokenhearted. "We never restricted her comings and goings with Troy. It isn't like she didn't have our approval to date him. He was always welcome here."

"I don't know, Vivian." Dad appears as dumbfounded as the rest of us. "I just don't know."

"Well, what was her reasoning?" Faith steps up to the plate and tosses a question in Dad's direction.

"She didn't have one, other than she loves him, and they felt it was the right time to get married."

"In high school? What did Troy have to say? Anything?" Faith blurts out my very thoughts.

"He said he loves her and will do whatever it takes to care for her," Mom says between tears.

"And you bought it?" I make myself known for the first time since entering the room.

"There isn't much we can do. In North Carolina, you don't need a parent's consent to get married at eighteen." Dad sounds so defeated. I hate them for doing this and ruining our birthday—heck, our lives. This is a day that will go down in infamy.

"So, now what?" I question, barely believing this is real life, not some cheesy soap opera.

"Well, we convinced Today to stay home until graduation in June. After that, if they decide to stay married, she can move out," Dad says, laying out his ultimatum. "Otherwise, we cut her off without any assistance with college, a car, or our support."

"And?" Faith says, questioning the outcome and our parent's sanity.

"And they agreed." The dark cloud hanging over Dad's office is palpable. The four of us sit in silence, digesting the day's events. "So, Today will live at home for the next five months; after that, she and Troy will live as husband and wife. God help us."

A cold chill runs down my spine because I know what kind of person Troy really is. Today needs to find out what a creep Troy is, but I don't see how that'll happen. She'll never believe anything I tell her.

God, please reveal the truth to my sister before graduation. Please don't let her ruin her life with that creep.

"Well, let's not let Tomorrow's eighteenth birthday be ruined by Today being so stupid and selfish." Faith stands to her feet, ever the optimist. "Let's go cut that gorgeous Oreo cake!"

The entire family looks in my direction, I assume to see if I'm up for the celebration. Oreo Cake from Asia's? Yes, please!

"Today is an idiot," Dad says, voicing the same exact thought in my brain. If she only knew what kind of jerk Troy is, she wouldn't still be with that ass, much less married him. I hope this is all a bad dream, but I know in my heart it's not.

"Did either of you have any idea she was up to something so stupid?" Mom asks sorrowfully, as she gets plates from the cupboard for the cake. I grab forks and napkins.

"I had no idea, but then again, she's always been the flighty one of the two." Faith is the first to respond, as she cuts a huge slice of cake and hands it to me. Faith tends to speaks first and think later, which is one of her most endearing qualities in my book.

"What about you, Tomorrow? Did you know anything about this stunt she's pulled?" Mom asks. All eyes are pointed at me.

"I had absolutely no idea. I'm as shocked as you guys are," I admit honestly. I realize that nobody sang Happy

Birthday to me today. and I miss my sister. We've never been apart on our birthday. I feel like half of me is missing. This birthday sucks, big time. *How, on God's green earth, has my world gone so crazy?* Everything is upside down and I don't like it one bit.

Nobody is in a festive mood. Mom plays with the slice of cake on her plate, pushing it from side to side, without taking a bite. Faith takes an unusually small slice, and Dad declines the cake altogether. This has turned out to be some birthday.

"I'm going to bed," Mom announces as she pushes back from the kitchen island. "Happy Birthday, sweetheart."

"Thanks, Mom. I love you."

"I love you too, kiddo."

I see the tear slide down her cheek as she gathers her plate and napkin. I can clearly see the pain on her face. It mirrors the pain in my heart.

11

"So, how was the traditional birthday dinner at Osha's last night?" Caleb inquires at Thanks A Latte. The coffee shop has been hopping since we opened at six a.m. However, three hours later, an unexpected but appreciated lull gave us a chance to breathe and restock before the college kids emerged from their slumber. I hear him but don't comprehend what he says to me. After last night's fiasco, my mind is elsewhere. "Did your mom get a buzz from the Thai Town Mules she loves so much?" he chuckles, aware that Mom is a lightweight, and can't have more than one drink without embarrassing herself in public. It's expected that plenty of laughter at her expense will ensue when we go to Osha's.

"I already refilled the sugar," I replied absently, wiping the same spot on the counter for the fifth time.

"Uhm, Tater, I didn't say anything about sugar," he says, touching my shoulder. Leaning in, he asks, "Are you okay?"

"Last night was a disaster," I confide in him. Unconsciously, I rub the 'Tater Bug' charm on the chain around my neck between my thumb and index finger. Caleb smiles at the sight of the charm, and I immediately let it drop.

"A disaster?" Caleb's eyebrows furrow. "What happened?"

"Today showed up with Troy."

"I thought it was a 'family only' affair," he said, making air quotes over his head.

"Well, surprise, Troy is part of the family now."

"What does that mean?"

"They waltzed into Osha's and Today flashed a diamond ring on her left hand. She skipped the customary chocolate chip pancake breakfast, and instead, she and Troy got married at city hall, to everybody's horror and surprise."

"You're kidding!"

"I wish I were kidding," I sigh, slumping on a barstool. The exhaustion of the previous twenty-four hours has caught up with me.

"Well, it isn't like everybody didn't already know they would end up getting married, right?" He sounds optimistic.

"Caleb, remember the night of the Homecoming dance?"

"Yeah…"

"Troy was the one that assaulted me." I unburden the last piece of my confession to Caleb. A sense of relief washes over me, but also fear, as I see his expression harden.

"*What?*" Caleb says, as shock registers on his features, and his fists clench. A muscle pops in his jaw, and I wonder if I made a mistake in telling him. "Why didn't you tell me earlier, Morrow? I can't believe this. I take it you haven't told your sister." Caleb is visibly upset. The pain is evident in his eyes, and I feel guilty for not telling him the truth sooner.

"No, I never told her. I didn't want to hurt her." I realize that by not telling her sooner, part of this fallout is my fault.

Had I told her from the beginning, she wouldn't have married that jerk. Now, it's too late. I've made a royal mess of things.

The bell over the door rings, signaling a customer has entered the shop. Caleb doesn't look toward the door; he stares at me. He's hurt and angry, but I can't tell which is the more dominant emotion. I can't seem to pull my eyes from his face, and I continue to hurt the people I care about with my silence. I can't win, no matter what action I take or don't take.

"What's a guy have to do to get some service around here?" A familiar voice chuckles, breaking the spell between Caleb and me.

Oh, my God. It's Troy.

"What the hell do you want?" Caleb shoots daggers at Troy with his tone.

"Whoa, what's up with you, man?" Troy plays the innocent party in this situation. "I want to order a couple of coffees to go." A machete couldn't cut through the tension in the shop right now.

Clutching Caleb's arm to keep him on our side of the counter, I glare at Troy. "There are other coffee shops besides this one. I suggest you go somewhere else to get your coffee," Caleb says through gritted teeth.

"What's your problem, man?"

"In a word...you." Caleb glares at Troy.

"Tomorrow, are you going to let this boy toy talk to your brother-in-law that way?" he winks at me. Troy's audacity is incredible.

"I think you should leave, Troy," I stammer as the bell chimes again.

Wesley's sister, Ashlynn, struts into Thanks A Latte, looking stunning in a puffy light blue parka, matching wool scarf, jeans, and cowboy boots. Her ice-blue eyes sparkle like the glistening shine in her hair.

"Tomorrow? Caleb? I didn't know you guys worked here. How cool is that?" Ashlynn says. She's a beautiful girl and by the looks on their faces, it's clear both Caleb and Troy agree.

"Tomorrow, will you introduce me to your friend?" Troy asks sweetly.

"Uhm..." I stutter, not wanting to make introductions.

"I'm Ashlynn," she extends her hand to Troy. "I just moved here from California." Her teeth are dazzling white as she smiles at Troy.

"Oh, nice to meet you. I'm Troy." He kisses the back of her hand. I gag, she swoons. Ashlynn seems impressed by Troy Whitaker, but I know he's merely a wolf in sheep's designer clothing.

"Can I get you something, Ashlynn?" Caleb asks, glaring once again at Troy. "Troy was just leaving. Weren't you?"

To my surprise, Troy doesn't make an issue out of Caleb's demand. "It was nice to meet you, Ashlynn. I hope to see you around soon," he schmoozes at her, then winks at me, glares at Caleb, and turns to leave.

"Tell Today we said hello," Caleb calls as Troy pushes through the door.

"Who was that?" Ashlynn inquires boldly with stars in her eyes.

"Nobody," Caleb and I say in unison.

~

THREE HOURS LATER, our shifts end. Caleb and I are sitting in Cricket. He's in the passenger seat, drumming his fingers against the dash, which grates my nerves. I hold on to the steering wheel like my car will launch into space unless I hold her down.

"Spill it, Tater." He wastes no time asking questions. "Why didn't you tell me it was that douchebag Troy that assaulted you?" Running his fingers through his hair, he blows out a disgusted breath. "I can't believe you didn't tell me. Me, of all people. I'm the one you can always confide in."

His voice is filled with as much hurt as it is anger. I don't know if he's madder at me or Troy. At this point, it doesn't matter. In my attempt to shield him, I ended up betraying his trust. I've gotten good at that these past six months—first my sister and now my closest friend. My life sucks. Period.

"I'm sorry, Caleb." I don't know what else to say, but I do what I can to explain. "Everything has gotten so messed up. I didn't want anyone to know it was him, especially Today. I thought maybe he was just drunk, or he thought I was Today, until he sent me that text and twisted everything around to Today, making it look like I wanted him." Resting my head on the steering wheel, I let the tears fall.

"Wait. What picture? What text?"

"Remember that day you were in my room, and Troy barged in?"

"Yeah..."

"Well, the next day, he sent me a text with a photo from Homecoming night when we were in his truck. The text said, 'I saw you and your little boy-toy in your room and am not pleased. Just know, Tomorrow Williams, you're mine.'"

"You've got to be joking, Tater."

"I wish." My eyes are red-rimmed and already swollen from crying. "The picture is misleading, though. It appears that I'm enjoying it. He showed it to Today and told her that I seduced him, and she believed him. She came into my room the next morning, smacked me in the face, and told me I would never have him. She hasn't spoken to me since." Tears flow like a torrent down my face. "God only knows why, but she married the bastard."

"That explains the 'boy-toy' comment earlier. But how did he get a picture?" Caleb thinks out loud.

"Today told me once that he has one of those dash cameras on his rearview mirror to record road rage and stuff to post on Facebook. I guess he turned it around."

"What an ass," Caleb comments, and I agree whole-heartedly. "Why didn't you tell me, Tater?"

"Because you're a second-degree black belt in karate, Caleb. I knew you would kick his butt. How would I explain that to Today? I was trying to keep the whole thing from her." Now, at this stage in the saga, my reasoning sounds weak, even to me.

"You're damn right. I would have kicked his butt." His knuckles turn white as his fists clench, and I know I need to calm him down. "And I will the next time I see that scumbag."

"Caleb, please don't," I plead. "He's married to my sister now, and she won't believe anything I tell her. How am I supposed to explain a fight between Troy and you? Besides, you'll probably end up putting him in the hospital...not that he doesn't deserve it."

"Well, for you, I won't fight him right now, but what is the deal with them getting married?"

"Who knows? They showed up last night at Osha's and said they got married. Mom and Dad freaked."

"Oh, I'll bet they did!"

"Dad talked Today into living at home until graduation by threatening to cut her off without a dime. Money talks, I guess." I almost laughed at that. "So, for the next five months, they'll live apart. If, after graduation, they want to continue this farce of a marriage, they will give their blessing."

"Did she explain anything to you or Faith?"

"Nope, she only said, 'You'll never get him now,' and slammed her door in my face. She believes the lie that I want Troy. God help me."

"Whoa, he has her brainwashed."

"Yup. She swallowed the blue pill."

"Here's what I don't get..." Caleb says after a long silence. "Why get married? He tells you that B.S. about you being 'his' but marries Today. How does that make any sense?" Resting his chin in his hands, brows furrowed in concentration, he vocalizes the same questions I've tossed around since the big marriage announcement yesterday. It isn't like I can ask my sister to explain.

"Your guess is as good as mine," I admit, defeated. "All I know is, he's nuts, and I can't shake the feeling that there's more to this drama than what's on the surface. He must have an angle or a reason to get married, but for the life of me, I can't figure it out."

"Only time will tell," Caleb reckons, shrugging his left shoulder.

"Yeah, and that scares the hell out of me."

"Has he tried to contact you again, besides that text with the picture?" he inquires. "Homecoming was in October. Were there any other incidents you haven't told me about in the past three months?" I hear the distrust in his voice, and it shatters me.

"No," I admit weakly.

"Tater Bug? Fess up," Caleb prods.

"I do my best to avoid Troy at all costs." I'm telling the truth, and I hope he believes me. "Sometimes, when he's at the house for dinner or picking up Today, I catch him looking at me, and he winks. It makes my skin crawl."

"He's such a creep."

"That's an understatement," I concur.

Caleb glances at his watch before asking, "Tater, are you okay? I'm worried about you. So much has happened in three months, and I'm afraid you can't handle it all."

"I'm fine," I lie. "I know God has a plan, and it'll all work out in the end."

"I don't know how you do it." Caleb lightly touches my right hand, and electricity runs up my arm. "You're so strong."

"I wonder if they give an Academy Award for the ultimate performance in real life, like they do for the big screen?" My smile is weak, but it's the best I can muster now.

"Well, in any event, I'm proud of you." His smile is so tender that my heart melts a little. "But if you ever need someone to talk to who is entirely unbiased, there *is* help out there for you." Smiling, he scribbles something on a piece of paper from his pocket and hands it to me.

"What's this?"

"It's my Aunt Kelly's email address. She told me I could give it to you if I thought you needed it. It might be a good idea to talk to her. She's one of those people with the gift of listening and helping others." His smile is so genuine. "If you don't reach out to her, please find someone else to talk to."

"Thanks, Caleb. You're the best," I say sincerely, leaning over to lay my head on his shoulder.

"Only for you, Tater Bug, only for you."

IT's 2:00 A.M., and I can't sleep. Tossing and turning in my bed has given me a migraine and a backache. Caleb's words keep echoing in my head, *'If you don't reach out to her, please find someone else to talk to.'*

Tossing my covers aside, I tiptoe to my desk but don't flip on the desk lamp. My laptop comes to life as I jiggle the mouse, the screen displaying a picture of Faith, Today, and myself at the beach last summer. It's the same picture I have framed on my nightstand. Opening my Gmail application, I type out an email to Caleb's aunt, outlining my sad set of circumstances and asking for advice. I've prayed for guidance, and this is the only offer of help that's been sent my way. I can only assume this is the direction God wants me to go in.

I've never met Kelly, but somehow, it's easier to be honest and bare my soul while hiding behind a screen. I start typing under the cover of darkness of my room.

To: Kelly F
From: Tomorrow W
Subject: Caleb's Messed-Up Friend

DEAR MRS. KELLY,

I KNOW that Caleb mentioned my "situation" to you, and I appreciate your offer of assistance. I'm lost and don't know where to turn for help. I can't talk to my youth pastor because my sister is in the same youth group, which would be awkward. Any advice would be most appreciated.

. . .

HERE IS *a brief recap of what you do or might know:*

In October, my twin sister's boyfriend sexually assaulted me at the Homecoming dance. Thank God, he did not rape me.

I NEVER TOLD MY SISTER, *thinking he might have been drinking and it would be a one-time thing. I couldn't bear to hurt her, so I kept the secret to myself, only telling Caleb what happened but not by whom.*

A FEW WEEKS LATER, *he texted me, saying, "I was his." Before I could tell my sister what happened, he lied to her and said I had come on to him. She believed him and turned against me. This, of course, has broken my heart. There was no point in telling her after he fed her all his lies; she would not believe me after what he told her happened. She won't speak to me now.*

THINGS YOU DON'T KNOW:

I am a virgin; Troy attempting to rape me has messed me up mentally. I have trust issues and nightmares; my emotions run the scale from sane to crazy, and my grades are suffering. But after all that, I still wanted to protect my sister from getting hurt and vowed to keep my secret.

CALEB NOW KNOWS *my sister's boyfriend, Troy, is the one who assaulted me.*

MY SISTER *and her boyfriend got married on our eighteenth*

birthday yesterday without telling anyone. I don't know why he married her.

MY DAD CONVINCED her to stay home until we graduated in May. If they wanted to remain married after graduation, he would continue to help pay for her college.

MY SISTER REFUSES to speak to me other than to sneer and say, "He's mine. Do you hear me? You'll never get your hands on him again. Forget we are sisters. As a matter of fact, forget you even know me. I will never speak to you again!"

MRS. KELLY, I am so confused, sad, and broken. I don't know what I should do from here. My sister made a huge mistake in marrying Troy, and I fear my silence led her to this irrational decision.

I'VE LOST MY SISTER. I'm trying to deal with this emotional rollercoaster on my own but failing miserably. I pray but hear no answers. Can you possibly give me some advice? I don't know what to do or where to turn.

ANY ADVICE WILL BE GREATLY APPRECIATED.

THANK YOU,
   Tomorrow Williams

． ． ．

READING BACK OVER THE EMAIL, it sounds professional, like a cover letter for a resume, and not the current state of my heart and sanity. I'm too emotionally drained to rewrite the email and quickly click 'send' before changing my mind.

Closing my laptop, I tread across the carpet and climb back into bed. Turning towards the window, I see the sun peek over the horizon. The day is dawning.

I hope that's a good sign.

12

Tammi, Bree, and I sit on the white carpet of my bedroom, surrounded by college brochures. We've yet to look at any of them seriously, but if Mom happens to pop in, she'll think we're having an in-depth conversation about where we will apply. My laptop is open in front of me to make it look good. In all actuality, we're gossiping about boys, school starting back tomorrow after Christmas break, and how much we dread the daily grind for the remaining semester of our senior year.

"Are you and Caleb applying to the same schools?" Bree asks innocently.

"What?" I choke on the Diet Dr. Pepper I'm drinking. "Why would we do that?"

"Oh, please," she tosses casually in my direction, rolling her eyes. "Of course, he'll follow you wherever you go. He's head over heels in love with you, Tomorrow. Everyone can see it except you," she says and picks up a brochure from Liberty University. "Lynchburg, Virginia?"

"Yeah, or Regent University in Virginia Beach. Both are close enough to come home but far enough not to come home." I give her a look that says I want out but not *out*. I need my space, especially after this crap with Troy, but I still want to be able to come home whenever I feel like it, without buying a plane ticket. "And both are Christian universities. Liberty is only a three-hour drive. Regent is only four hours. Both are doable in Cricket."

"True," Bree agrees, "But I want to go as far from here as possible. I'm applying to party schools like LSU, WVU, and UCLA. I submitted my applications over Christmas break," she says, her eyes sparkling. Oh yeah, she wanted to party her way through college.

"Tammi, what about you?" Bree asks. I already know the answer to this question, as Tammi and I've discussed college on many occasions.

"Oh, I don't think I'm going to college," she admits sheepishly. "Jeremy and I have been discussing long-term plans, and college doesn't seem to be in the picture for me." Her eyes gloss over dreamily. It's no secret that they are in it for the long haul. I couldn't be happier for her. "I want to be a stay-at-home wife and mother. Jeremy wants the same for his future wife. So, we are on the same page about our life-long dreams."

"Uhm, is there something you aren't telling us?" Bree and I lock eyes momentarily and then turn to Tammi.

"No, nothing is set in stone yet." She wriggles her eyebrows. "But hopefully, after graduation, that will change."

The morning, filled with friends, fun, and laughter, passes swiftly. My mood lifts, and I enjoy spending time with my besties. The only one missing is Caleb, but he wouldn't like all the gossip and the talk about boys, him being one of them. Carly isn't here either, but we all know her time is filled with Wesley, which is okay with us.

Boyfriends, potential or permanent, always trump a gossip session.

"Carly has been spending quite a bit of time with Wesley lately. I haven't seen her too much over the break," Tammi said, referring to our missing comrade.

"If she isn't with Wes, she's with his sister, Ashlynn," Bree offers flippantly, and I can't help but wonder if there isn't a bit of jealousy in her tone. Bree is the confident one, always appearing comfortable around guys at school, always the center of attention. A happy, smiling, and accomplished flirt, but now I wonder if that isn't all an act. I'm not nearly as outgoing and bubbly as Bree, but I'm hiding behind a mask, concealing a secret only a few know. Is Bree doing the same?

"I like Ashlynn. I've only been around her a few times, but I like her," I say. "I'm sure the guys at school will like her, too." Caleb and Troy flash through my mind simultaneously, causing conflicting emotions to swirl in my gut like a tornado. I don't want either of them to be attracted to the beautiful blonde but for different reasons.

"School should be interesting tomorrow when she struts into the cafe before the first bell," Bree says sardonically. I don't have a comeback that I can vocalize, but my mind is abuzz with different scenarios of how the following day will unfold. Looking at my friends, it appears they're doing the same.

"Well, let's invite her to sit at our table to ward off the vultures," Tammi suggests, always the protective one. She'll make a great mom one day. She has that motherly instinct, which has been evident since the sand incident in the second grade. "I'm sure she'll be nervous on the first day at a new school, and I know Carly will appreciate it."

"I don't know, Tammi," Bree challenges. "I don't think we should do that yet."

"Why not?" Tammi asks in an uncertain tone.

"We don't even know this girl. She could be some serial killer escaping arrest by the cops in California." Bree blurts out the most absurd reason imaginable. "I mean, everything is fake on her, from her nails to her hair color. We don't know anything about her."

"Oh, my goodness, Bree." I'm astonished at her reaction to inviting Ashlynn to join our group in the cafeteria. "Where's this paranoia coming from?"

THE WEATHER IS DARK, cold, and gloomy, and black clouds fill the skies the next day at school. You would never know it by the scene inside the cafeteria, which is abuzz with the roar of students reunited with their friends after the holiday break. Laughter and conversation can be heard echoing from wall to wall. Formica tables fill with their usual groups of students. Jocks sit by the windows, tossing footballs and basketballs to one another as cheerleaders swarm the seated athletes; the nerds and bookworms occupy the tables nearest the food bar; stoners crouch together in the corner furthest away from the entrance doors; and the rest of the student body fill in the remaining tables in the cafeteria. My friend group, consisting of Tammi, Jeremy, Bree, Carly, Caleb, and I, occupy the table in the center of the dining hall.

The heavy gray double doors of the cafeteria open wide, and an unusual hush falls over the student body. Ashlynn has entered, and every head turns in her direction. She sashays into the room like Marilyn Monroe, with a seductive smile and a glint in her eye. She looks fantastic in a tight, light blue wool sweater that accentuates her eyes (and her boobs), a tight pair of jeans that she must have poured herself into, along with a pair of heeled boots. Every set of eyes is on her, causing several girlfriends to smack their boyfriends on the shoulder to distract them from the beautiful blonde that has joined the Holly Springs High School ranks.

"She sure knows how to make an entrance," I whisper to Tammi. It doesn't escape my notice that Caleb needs to pick his jaw up from the floor. It isn't like he hasn't seen her before.

"I'll say," Bree responds to my comment. I notice, however, that she isn't looking at Ashlynn; she's looking across the cafeteria in the direction of Today and Troy. She scowls and curls her lip in displeasure. "She thinks she's all that and a bag of chips."

"Bree?" I ask," Are you talking about Ashlynn or someone else?" Curiosity has grabbed ahold of me now. Why is she looking at my sister when we are supposedly talking about Ashlynn?

"Oh, uh, Ashlynn, of course," she answers, but I'm unconvinced. I believe something's rotten in the state of Denmark.

Ashlynn heads toward our table, not phased by the commotion she caused by entering the food court. Being from California, I guess she's used to causing a ruckus. *Wow, what a stereotypical thought on my part. Oh well, it is what it is.* Ashlynn has the typical California look that makes others jealous, me being one of them. I felt somewhat pretty and attractive in the past, but that all changed thanks to Troy. I don't know how, but because of that encounter with him, I feel worthless, ugly, and not worth a dime to anyone. I've never been conceited, but I did feel relevant and vital as student body president. I've entirely let those duties slide during the first semester of school, to the point that I'll be resigning. It's a no-brainer. More will be expected of me in the spring. And I dread prom season.

"Hi, guys!" Ashlynn smiles as she sits at our table, right between Caleb and me. *Uhm, excuse me?* She's either bold or extremely self-confident, inserting herself between us. Shouldn't she be sucking up to Carly? She's practically Wes's girlfriend, and Carly invited her to sit with us. Caleb scoots closer, and a slight smile creeps across my lips.

"Hey, Ashlynn," Carly says. "How has your first morning been?" The rest of us mumble a random greeting.

"It's been great! I've met so many nice people," she says, beaming. "Caleb and I have trig together first period."

"Really?" I sneer at Caleb. "Your favorite subject?" We all laugh. It's common knowledge that he hates all things math related. I get a text about trig from him daily.

"I was thinking we could study together a few evenings a week," Ashlynn purrs in his direction. "Whatddya say?"

"I don't know. With work and stuff, I'm pretty busy." He looks to me for help. "Tater here is the math wiz. She has already taken trig and aced it last year."

Way to throw me under the bus, chump, I think to myself. He knows I hate tutoring. But, ever the polite one, I suggest, "Why don't we all get together one night a week at Thanks A Latte and study as a group? Finals will be here before we know it and I'm sure Vickie won't mind." Sometimes I'm a genius.

"Sounds good to me," Tammi and Jeremy speak up in unison.

"I'm in," Carly chimes in.

"Bree? What about you?" Tammi asks. Yet again, I notice

that Bree isn't engaged in our conversation but continues to stare at my sister across the cafeteria. What's up with her today?

"What?" Bree says, surfacing from her surveillance. "Oh, yeah, sure."

"Bree? Are you okay?" My question gets cut short by a loud *buzz buzz buzz*. The fire alarm sounds as smoke bellows from the kitchen. Everyone rushes to different exits from the cafeteria in a mad dash of confusion. Girls are screaming, guys are yelling, and everyone scrambles to grab their cell phones, purses, backpacks, and the like. It's total pandemonium—so much for the fire drills we've rehearsed since elementary school. My instincts kick in, and I search frantically for my sister to ensure we get to safety together. The cafeteria is rapidly filling with smoke. Caleb grabs my hand as I struggle to find Today in the frenzy of students.

"I saw them go that way." He points to a side door that leads to the quad. He knows me so well. I see her with Troy as they slip outside. She didn't look back for me or give my safety a second thought. She really does hate me. "Come on," he says, pulling me toward the same door Today and Troy had dashed through just a moment earlier, but I pull him in the other direction. She doesn't care about my safety; I won't care about hers. "This way," I yell over the chaos and drag him to another exit.

"Tater, where are you going?" He objects since we're at the closest way to the safety of the quad.

"Tammi and the others went to the south side," I protest. My throat and lungs begin to burn from the smoke filling the lunchroom, and it's getting harder to see where I'm headed. More than once, I bump into a table and stumble. Caleb never releases my hand as we navigate the labyrinth left behind by the surging mass of kids racing to the outside world. My breathing is labored, and my eyes burn; a rancid smell mixes with the black billows of smoke still pouring from the kitchen at the back of the cafeteria, which is the precise direction I'm pulling Caleb in.

"Tomorrow! Stop!" I hear the panic in his voice, but I keep going in the opposite direction of my sister. "Where are you going? We gotta get out of here!" But I'm a woman on a mission and I ignore him. I'm determined to get to the opposite side of the school—far away from my sister.

The smoke is blacker than night, the fire alarm is still ringing, blaring through the frenzy. The smoke is filling my lungs more and more with each breath. Frantically, I turn around, lost in the smoke. I don't know where I am or which way it is to the nearest exit. I've been in this cafeteria a billion times, yet I find myself lost in a strange place. I can't breathe. I can't see. I can't think. Then—I succumb to the smoke and crumble to the floor.

"TOMORROW!" Caleb screams my name. The only thought I have as I free fall to the floor is that *most deaths in a fire occur from smoke inhalation.* We all learned that in the fifth grade when the fire department visited our class to teach about fire safety. Caleb is screaming my name, but his voice fades into the background. Abruptly, as if hitting a wall, everything fades to black.

I'm vaguely aware of Caleb as he lifts me off the ground and carries me towards the closest exit. Despite feeling disoriented by the thick smoke surrounding us, he stumbles out of the cafe with me in his arms. It's like a dream, coming in and out of consciousness. This is a dream from which I don't want to wake. It feels nice being in his arms.

"Tomorrow Williams, don't you leave me." Caleb's voice echoes in the space between my ears. I try to grasp the words, to catch them in my hands, but they elude me.

"Tater Bug, do you hear me?" The cloud I'm adrift on is soft and warm. I want to stay here. Today intrudes into the realm of my unconscious and I want to call to her, but the fog is too thick. She looks at me and vanishes. She never comes close enough to embrace; she only stares and then is gone. "Tomorrow!" Caleb's voice reaches the cortex of my brain, and then he vanishes, too. I'm alone in my darkness.

Reaching the safety of outside, I assume Caleb performed CPR on me. When I come back to consciousness; Caleb's lips are on mine. Gasping for air, I try to sit up, but my head spins. I have no strength. My arms feel like lead pipes; my legs feel like they are buried in sand.

"Whoa, whoa, whoa," Caleb clutches me to his chest. "Don't try to sit up. The fire department and paramedics are on the way." Sirens blare in the distance as Caleb lowers my back to the cold, hard ground, but he doesn't release his hold on me. I shiver in the cold January air. At least, I think it's from the temperature...or is it from Caleb's touch?

"Tomorrow? Are you okay?" Tammi drops to her knees beside me. "We couldn't find you. I thought we all went out the south door, but when I turned, you were gone." Tears run down her cheeks, streaking the soot covering her face. Carly, Bree, and Jeremy stand behind Tammi but don't get too close.

"She pulled me toward the other side of the cafeteria to get out," Caleb explains simply. I suppose that's because he doesn't have anything else to offer. There was no time for explanations; I just had to get away from Today and Troy. In doing so, I put myself and Caleb in danger. I could never forgive myself if anything had happened to Caleb because of my stupidity and pride.

"Thank God, you're both ok," Carly sighs, clearly

relieved. "Wait, where's Ashlynn? Wasn't she with us when we got to the quad?"

"Yeah, I saw her," Jeremy offers. "She made it out with that guy, Austin Sheldon." He tilts his head to the right, indicating where Ashlynn and Austin are standing. "She looks okay to me."

"Oh, thank God," Carly says, visibly relieved that her boyfriend's sister is okay. "She's had an incredible first day at Holly Springs High. I hope she doesn't expect this much excitement every day!"

"No doubt," Bree says for the first time. "This is the most excitement we've had around here in forever."

"This excitement, I can do without," Tammi proclaims. The rest of my friends agree.

"Is there anyone here in distress from the smoke?" An EMT enters my circle of friends and sees me lying on the ground. "This must be the patient." The paramedic kneels beside me, gives me a reassuring fatherly smile, and puts an oxygen cannula under my nose. "Can everyone step back, please? Let's give this lady some room to breathe."

"I'm not going anywhere," Caleb informs the EMT authoritatively. He means business.

"Aww, you must be this beauty's boyfriend." He chuckles like Santa Claus. He seems almost jolly. Wait, Christmas was last month. Right?

"Something like that," Caleb doesn't sound in a joking mood. "Just...is she going to be okay?"

The paramedic checks my blood pressure, listens to my heart and lungs with his stethoscope, checks for dilation and responsiveness of my pupils, and asks me some absurd questions.

"Young lady, what's your name?

"Tomorrow Williams."

"What year is it?"

"2024"

"Do you know why I'm here?"

"There was a fire in the cafeteria. Caleb saved me."

"Son," the medic addressed Caleb, "She'll be fine. Her breathing is normal, her lungs are clear, she's coherent, and she isn't coughing any longer."

"Oh, thank God," I can hear the relief in his voice. "Can I take her home, or does she need to go to the ER for further evaluation?"

I feel like I'm in an episode of *Grey's Anatomy*.

St. Nick turns his attention back to me. "How are you feeling, dear? Can you sit up?"

Nodding my head to reassure everyone that I'm on the mend, I sit up. Granted, the scenery sways slightly, but I can sit upright. "I'm feeling better. Thank you so much, sir."

"Now, let this fine young man take you home, drink plenty of fluids, and get some rest." He winks at me. "If you feel bad again, go straight to the emergency room. Okay?"

"I promise."

The paramedic leaves, and Caleb helps me get to my feet. I'm feeling much better but a little tired. My throat is scratchy, and I smell like a smokestack. I give hugs to Tammi, Carly, and Bree, and I'm thankful for my friends who love and care about me so much. That's more than I can say for my twin sister. *Selfish bitch,* I think.

"I'm going to head home and take a shower," I tell my group, turning toward the parking lot and Cricket.

"Uhm, no, you don't, Tater Bug," Caleb insists. "The EMT specifically told me to take you home. We can get your car later."

I'm not in the mood to argue. I'll lose anyway. When he decides to do something, his mind doesn't change.

"Fine."

"You stay right here; I'll go get the Stang. Tammi, don't let her leave. I'll be right back." He hands me off to my best girlfriend and disappears.

"That boy loves you, Tomorrow." Her voice is honeyed in my ear. "You know that, right?"

I just roll my eyes at her and refuse to answer. Regardless of my feelings toward Caleb, I know he doesn't want a soiled dove.

OUR PRINCIPAL DISMISSED classes for the remainder of the day after the fire department gave the 'all clear' sign, and left the school property. Tammi's words bounce around in my brain later that afternoon as I try to nap. Caleb is a stand-up guy, but even he has his limits. Another guy fondling my breasts and taking pictures is too much to ask any guy to overlook, even Caleb. Life has become a rollercoaster of emotions these past few months. Beginning with Troy's attack, to my wasted attraction to Caleb, Today marrying that liar, and finally, the fire today at school. I feel like my heart is about to explode sometimes.

I can hear Today rummaging around in her room around midnight. She didn't knock on my door to check if I had made it safely home from school. I can see her clearly in my mind as she turns off her Alexa, playing nineties country and flipping off her light. Listening intently, hoping to hear our ritualistic goodnight taps of *one-three-one*, but no sounds came through the darkness. I tapped on the wall instead of waiting an eternity for her to knock. *One-three-one*. Again, I waited for her reply of two knocks. They never came. Pulling the covers over my head, tears began to slip down my cheek. My heart remains shattered.

13

"Are you serious?" Tammi is astonished at my admission of Today's silence for the past month. "She hasn't spoken to you since your birthday?"

"Nope, not a word to me. She does speak to Mom and Dad when she's home but avoids me like I have smallpox or something." My voice is brittle with emotion. I miss my sister, but I can't do anything about it. She's turned the cold shoulder into an art form.

"What do your parents say? Surely, they've noticed."

"If they've noticed, they haven't mentioned it. They usually let us work out our differences without interfering." This time, however, I wish they would. "Hey, remember I told you about Caleb's aunt in Hickory? The Stephen Minister?"

"Oh, yeah. Stephen Ministers are counselors, right?" She asks, tilting her head to one side. She's so cute sometimes.

"From what I understand, they are more like, uhm, someone to help you walk through troublesome times in your life, I guess." I do my best to explain from the email I received from Mrs. Kelly a few weeks ago. "You meet with them once a week, and they help you work through issues, pray with and for you, and offer insight from the Bible. It's all confidential, so I'm told."

"That sounds great. Have you met with one yet?"

"No, I emailed her last month, and she told me she can hook me up with a Stephen Minister from a church here in Holly Springs, but I haven't responded to her yet," I confess, feeling guilty about that, too.

"Why not?" Tammi sounds mildly irritated that I have stalled getting some help. "What does Caleb think about it?"

"He doesn't know, and I don't think his aunt would tell him anything, anyway." Which is a relief on my part. Either Mrs. Kelly kept the emails between us, or Caleb is letting me do this alone. Either way, I'm thankful I'm not being pressured. They seem to be letting me move at my own pace. At this point, my pace is slower than a turtle. "I don't know if I can tell what happened to me to a stranger, ya know?"

"Maybe a total stranger is exactly what you need, Tomorrow," Tammi says, touching my arm lovingly. "Don't try to cope with all this mess on your own. Maybe you need someone not so close to the situation to give some perspective. A Stephen Minister sounds like just what you need." Her smile is soft and genuine. Maybe, just maybe, she's right.

Just thinking about it makes my heart pound and my palms get clammy. I don't like talking to strangers and talking about what Troy did seems unthinkable. All these thoughts swirl in my mind, making me woozy. Rubbing the 'Tater Bug' charm between my thumb and forefinger has a calming effect. I find myself doing it a lot. Slowly, I respond, "I'll think about it, okay?"

"Okay," she agrees and gives me a warm hug. I don't

know what I would do without Tammi. She's always there for me, no matter what, and I love her for it.

"Hey," I say, changing the subject away from me. "Have you noticed anything odd about Bree lately?"

"Not really," Tammi says as she takes Penelope out of her cage and strokes her soft black-and-white fur. "Why?"

"I don't know; she just seems... different." I can't quantify her behavior; it seems off since we returned to school after Christmas break. Notably, the day of the fire at school. "The day the cafeteria caught on fire, I noticed she kept staring at Today with Troy. It was weird."

'Hmm..." Tammi seemed to ponder my statement before responding. "Now that you mention it, she has been distant. I assumed she was busy with cheerleading since basketball season is starting up. Do you think something is going on? Maybe a new man she hasn't told us about?"

"I don't know," I reply honestly, hoping it has nothing to do with Troy. "Maybe it's just my imagination. She's probably just been busy."

"I'll pay more attention," Tammi offers. "I'm sure it's nothing."

"Yeah, you're probably right." I think my mistrust of Troy has overtaken my rational thought process, making me suspicious of the simplest things. "Make sure you lock Penelope's cage when you put her back. Faith almost killed me last time she got loose."

"DAD, I want to buy Today's half of Cricket," I announce matter-of-factly as I enter his study.

"Uhm, okay." His brow crinkles as he questions my sudden interest in the car. "Why?"

"Well, she's 'married' now," I say and make exaggerated air quotes. "Let Troy buy her a car. Besides, she's never here, and when she has Cricket all day and into the night, I have no access to her."

"Well, you'll have to ask your sister about that. If she agrees, we'll negotiate a fair price. Okay?" My dad is always the diplomat.

"You might need to do that on my behalf. Today isn't exactly speaking to me right now," I confess.

"I've noticed that," Mom states from the doorway. I didn't realize she was listening. "What's going on with you two?"

My mind races. All my responses to this question evaporate into thin air. I thought I was prepared for when one of my parents, or Faith, asked this question. "I mean," I stammer. "She's rarely here, that's all." I pray my excuse is believable, even if the execution isn't perfect.

"Hmm..." Mom murmurs. I don't think she's buying it, but she doesn't press. "We'll talk to your sister."

"How much is half, anyway?" I probably should have asked before I offered to buy Today out. I have some money in my savings account, but I'm not loaded by any means.

"We can discuss a price if she agrees to the deal, okay?" Dad offers. "I'll let you know."

"Thanks, Dad." I kiss him on the cheek. "You're the best."

Their discussion continues as I exit Dad's study, but in hushed tones. I have no doubt they're discussing the tension between Today and myself. I can't offer them any explanation other than the one I gave. As I ascend the stairs to my room, I try to push the situation out of my mind, without any success.

· · ·

DEAR MRS. KELLY,

I'M sorry I haven't gotten back to you sooner. I wasn't sure I was ready to speak to a stranger about my situation, but things haven't gotten any better in my head after the incident.

I thought I would be over it by now, four months later. Turns out I was wrong.

I WOULD GREATLY APPRECIATE it if you could help me find a Stephen Minister in Holly Springs.

THANK YOU SO MUCH,
Tomorrow

~

IT'S A FRIGID SATURDAY MORNING, even for February. The thermometer outside the kitchen window reads 39°F and the windows are fogged over. I might need two cups of coffee to warm me up before I head out to work. Cricket is warming up in the driveway. Except for Christmas, I'm not much of a winter person. I hate being cold. Then again, I hate being hot, too, so summer isn't my favorite time of year, except when I'm in the pool. Spring and autumn suit me perfectly. Caleb says I'm a lukewarm kind of person. I'm not sure if that's a compliment or an insult. But, all in all, he isn't wrong. I'm most comfortable in the middle. I don't do well in the extremes. I ponder this dimension of my personality as I stare out at the dead trees of winter, sipping my hot beverage. Winter is ugly unless there's snow on the ground. Snow is a rare sight here in Holly Springs.

"How long will you be in here?" Today asks from the doorway, "I'll come back."

"Today, don't leave." I'm shocked by her appearance in the kitchen. First, I didn't know she was home, but I was even more surprised when she actually spoke to me. I've missed the sound of her voice. "Please, don't leave."

"Fine," she says indignantly. "Dad says you want to buy my half of Cricket. Is that so?" Ice drips from her tone, which is colder than the temperature outside the window.

"Uhm, yeah." I had hoped our first conversation in weeks would have had more substance than discussing the sale of a car, but I'll take what I can get. "It only makes sense that one of us has full-time access to her, and you are always with Troy anyway." I hate saying his name out loud, and I'm actually nervous about talking to my twin. *Life has gone loco!*, I think to myself.

"Five thousand, non-negotiable," she spits out. "Take it or leave it. You have ten seconds to decide."

She knows how much I have in my savings account and is willing to wipe it out completely. I'm astonished at how coldhearted she has become toward me. This isn't the Today Williams, uhm, Today Whitaker, with whom I shared a womb. Swallowing hard and choking back a tear, I agree. "Okay, five thousand."

"Fine. When you give Dad the cash, the car is yours." She turns to leave and says over her shoulder, "That makes us done."

Sitting on the barstool at the island, I stare into my mug of coffee, replaying the conversation in my mind. The front door slams behind her, and she's gone again. *God, why is this happening? I'm the victim here, but Today thinks I'm the enemy. Please step in and resolve this before I lose my sister forever,* I pray to myself. Glancing at the clock on the microwave, I realize it's time to get ready for work. I really don't want to go to work now.

My phone chimes from my nightstand in the other room as I apply the last touch of mascara to my lashes. I don't have time to chat this morning, but I read it while sitting in *my* car as she warms up. It's a text from Carly. She's up early on a Saturday.

Carly: *Are you going to the Valentine's Day Ball?*

Tomorrow: *No, I don't think so. Are you going?*

Carly: *Yes! Wesley asked me today! Aren't you going with Caleb?*

Tomorrow: *That's great! Why does everybody always assume we will go to dances together?*

Carly: *You are clueless, Girl. It's as plain as the nose on your face. That boy is nuts about you.*

Tomorrow: *No, you are nuts! I gotta go. I am heading to work. TTYL*

Carly: *Mmhmm. Bye =)*

I END the text before Carly gets carried away and plans an elaborate scheme to get Caleb and I to go together to the ball. The last thing I need is to go to another dance after the last incident. I pray Caleb doesn't ask me to go (even just as friends) and that my girlfriends won't pursue this endeavor to get us together as a couple. They have no idea how impossible that will be. I throw Cricket into reverse and back out of the driveway. Time to go to work.

~

THANKS A LATTE is crowded this morning. It must be the cold, dismal weather. I am so ready for spring. I long for green grass, trees budding, flowers blooming, warmer temperatures, and, most importantly, graduation! Goodbye, high school. It's hard to believe that everything in my life will change again in four short months. I'm not sure I can handle it, but willing to try.

"Hey, Tater Bug," Caleb calls across the coffee shop as I walk in. I have concluded that Tater Bug is his favorite nickname for me. I admit, I like it.

I know he isn't scheduled this morning. I was a little bummed when Vickie posted the schedule for the weekend. Caleb and I generally work Saturday mornings together, but I work with Victor this weekend. He's a stuffed shirt without a sense of humor. It's going to be a long shift. Looking in Caleb's direction, questions pelt my brain. Why is Caleb sitting cozily at a corner table with Ashlynn? My stomach churns, and I throw up a little in my mouth. Caleb and Ashlynn? I know she's flirted with him at school, but I've never seen him return the affection.

I wave a quick hello, but Caleb doesn't see my greeting. He's already turned his attention back to Ashlynn and whispers something that makes her giggle. I don't know why I expected anything different from Caleb. Sure, we're best friends, but that's as far as it goes. Any hopes of our relationship developing into anything further got dashed by Troy. Caleb knows too much to want anything to do with me other than friendship. I'm not girlfriend material any longer. *Thanks, Troy.*

The coffee shop is busy, and I find it difficult to keep one eye on Caleb and Ashlynn, and the other on the customer in front of me. I'm surprised at my reaction to Caleb talking to another girl. We're just friends, after all, but I can't help feeling a little green with envy. My feelings for Caleb run deeper than I thought.

"Earth to Tomorrow," Victor calls to get my attention. "How long are you going to froth that milk? The line is backing up." Snapping back to the task at hand, I realize the milk is beyond frothed, if that's possible. *Pull it together, Tomorrow.*

"Oh, sorry," I apologize and return to making the latte ordered. Victor merely grunts and turns back to the counter. The line is getting longer, and I need to concentrate on my customers.

"Bye, Tater," Caleb calls as he and Ashlynn leave the shop. My heart sinks a little as I watch Caleb hold the door for Ashlynn and place his hand on the small of her back, as they walk through the glass door. Not ten seconds after Caleb and Ashlynn are out of my field of vision, Troy walks into the store. Can this day get any worse?

"What are you doing in here?" I spit at Troy as he approaches the counter. "You are NOT welcome here."

"Whoa, calm down, Morrow. Aren't you happy to see your new brother-in-law?" His smirk is repulsive and makes my stomach churn.

"Haven't you caused enough trouble in my family?" Speaking to him takes every ounce of self-control I can muster. I want to jump across the counter and scratch his eyes out.

"Tomorrow, you were the one I wanted to ask out our freshman year instead of your sister, but I could see you were all starry-eyed over that punk Caleb." He plays the pitiful act well, but I'm not buying it.

"Get out of here, Troy," I demand. Victor flashes me a

wary look; he has no idea what's happening within my family unit. "I have nothing to say to you after the lies you told my sister. She isn't speaking to me because she thinks I want you—as if!"

"Yeah, I was thinking that could work to our advantage." He glances around the shop conspiratorially. "Since Today already thinks you want me, we can prove her right." His eyes light up at his 'brilliant' plan. Oh my God, this guy is sick.

"What the heck are you talking about? I don't want anything to do with you!"

"But Today doesn't know that," he says as he waggles his eyebrows.

"Troy, get out of here." My voice lowers an octave to a threatening tone. I wish Caleb were here to protect me against Troy. Victor is worthless.

"Troy? What are you doing here?" Today barges through the glass door. "And why are you talking to *her*?"

"Hi, Babe. I came in to surprise you with that Southern Belle latte you love so much. I didn't know Tomorrow was working," he says with choirboy innocence. "Why are you here? You ruined my surprise." Today is buying his lie. I can tell because her face melts from anger to adoration in 2.2 seconds.

"I saw your truck outside." She sneers in my direction, "I'm sorry you had to see *her* this morning."

"Yeah, can you believe she asked me out again?" Troy's lies flow so fluidly he could be a lawyer. "She has no respect for our marriage, babe." Troy kisses her on the cheek. "Let's get out of here."

"I most certainly did not!" I shout in their faces. "You asked me out!"

"You're pathetic, Tomorrow," Today glares before they

walk out, arm in arm. As Today and Troy leave the coffee shop, I notice a piece of paper fall out of Troy's pocket. Curiosity gets the best of me. Racing across the room, I pick up the paper and unfold it. The crumpled paper has Bree's phone number on it. *What the crap? Why does he have Bree's number?*, I think to myself.

14

"Penelope, what am I going to do?" I ask the fluffball in my lap. She doesn't offer any advice but does give me comfort. Faith has had her pet skunk for as long as I can remember. She's a part of almost every childhood memory I have. I was so happy she didn't take her to college with her. I don't think her boyfriend, Hunter, is fond of Penelope. That suits me just fine. My cellphone chimes with an incoming email, so I give Pen one last nuzzle, a piece of cucumber, and put her back in her cage. She's one spoiled skunk.

The email is from an address I don't recognize, but the subject heading catches my attention: Stephen Ministry. Hesitantly, I open the email.

Hello, Tomorrow,

My name is Sierra Miller. I am a Stephen Minister at Mill-brook United Methodist Church in Raleigh. Kelly Folger emailed me to explain your situation with your sister and new husband. I am in my early twenties, and Kelly felt I could relate to your age and situation. I would love to meet to talk.

A Stephen Minister is a lay member of a congregation trained to provide one-on-one care to someone going through difficult times. Our congregation's Stephen Leaders equip us with caring ministry skills and train us to listen, care for, and walk with people. A Stephen Minister provides emotional and spiritual support for people experiencing grief, divorce, job loss, chronic or terminal illness, relocation, or traumatic events in their lives that they are having issues dealing with (as in your situation with your sister).

I cannot solve your problems, but I can guide you using biblical principles to help you cope with the trauma you are dealing with.

I would love to meet in person, but we can begin by texting if you prefer. I hope to hear from you soon.

Trusting in Him,

Sierra

I CLOSE the email to ponder the situation. This is all new to me. I like the fact that she's from Raleigh and not Holly Springs. She wouldn't know my sister or any of my friends. We're close to the same age, and I know I need someone to talk to. I can't keep living this way; I'm slowly losing my mind. Maybe she will understand what I am dealing with. I can always stop talking to her if I'm uncomfortable, right? I talk to myself more and more these days. I hope I give myself good advice. Before I change my mind, I type out a quick reply from my iPhone:

Sierra,

Thank you for your email. I would very much like to meet with you to talk. Can we possibly meet at Jitter Bean in Garner on Saturday morning? If that isn't good, pick a time and place, and I will be there.

Here is my phone number: 919-555-6459.

Thanks,
Tomorrow

WITHIN SECONDS, my cellphone dings with a text message:
Sierra: *I'll see you Saturday morning at about 9 a.m.*
Tomorrow: *I'll be there.*

"TOMORROW?" Mom calls from the kitchen. "Can you come down here, please?" Her tone is too sweet for me to be in trouble; besides, I can't think of anything I've done wrong lately. Of course, that doesn't mean anything.

"Sure, Mom, I'll be right there," I yell down the stairs as I pull on my favorite Holly Springs High sweatpants and hoodie. The weather is getting warmer now that it's mid-March, but I'll take any excuse to wear my sweats.

"What's up?" I ask. Mom and Dad are sitting at the kitchen island with steaming mugs of coffee. "Is something wrong?"

"Of course not, sweetheart," Mom coos. "We have a surprise for you."

"For me?" Excitement fills my voice. "What is it?"

"Well," Dad begins, "We're proud of you for saving your money to purchase your sister's half of the Volkswagen, so we decided to put the title in your name. She is officially yours." Dad hands me the title to the black Beetle in the driveway. "And we are returning half the money you paid for the bug. I don't know why Today was being selfish with the price. I guess she thought the cash would go to her." Dad snickered.

"Oh, my goodness," I gush. "That's so sweet! Thank you

guys so much." I stare at the official NC title in my hands. She's all mine. Nobody (specifically Today) can take her from me now. I haven't been this giddy in a long time. I want to run right out and wash her now.

"But wait, there's more," Mom says, sounding like a late-night infomercial. "We got you a personalized tag, too."

"You did what?" I say, astonished.

"We sure did," Dad says, beaming from ear to ear, and hands me the envelope the license plate is nestled in. Slowly, I remove the new tag from the envelope and tear up.

"Oh, wow!"

The plate reads TATERBUG.

"Caleb came up with the tag."

"Of course, he did." I laugh, clutching the plate to my chest.

"Dad, will you put my tag on for me, please? I want to go show Tammi." I'm giddy inside. I can't wait for my friends to see it. My second stop will be Thanks A Latte. I know Caleb is working, and I want to thank him for his suggestion to my parents.

"Oh, I love it!" Tammi exclaims as she inspects my car's newly acquired license plate. "I guess she is no longer Cricket, huh?"

"Nope, that ship has sailed. Tater Bug is all mine now." I beam with pride like a new parent.

"It's funny, though," Tammi muses, "Doesn't the charm on your necklace say the same thing?"

"Yeah, what's your point?" I mock defensiveness. I know where she is headed with this line of questioning.

"My point is this: Didn't Caleb give you that charm for

Christmas?" her raised eyebrow speaks volumes to her indication. "This can't be a coincidence."

"He might have suggested a vanity plate to my mom."
Wow, I'm blushing. I can feel the warmth creep up my
cheeks.

"I told you how that boy feels about you, Tater Bug," she
says, my nickname heavily emphasized.

"Oh, hush, you!" I toss a Kleenex in her direction. "Let's
go to Thanks A Latte. Caleb is working, and I want to show
off the new plate."

"You know his schedule, too?" The lilt in her voice is
unmistakable. I imagine she's writing a Hallmark special in
her mind already.

"Get in," I admonish, laughing all the while.

"Hey, can we run by Veteran's Park first?" she inquires. "I
want to put some books in the Little Free Library by the
workout course."

"Sure, it's great that you always donate books there."
Tammi has such a kind heart. I admire her for that.

"Yeah, I read a great book, *Frankie*, last week, and I want
to share." She holds up the paperback, the cover of which is
beautiful and mysterious.

"Maybe I'll read it sometime."

"Pfft," she spits. "The only thing you ever read is that
worn-out copy of *Pride and Prejudice* that Caleb gave you."

"Wow, you are on it today, aren't you?"

She smiles and shrugs her shoulder. "Maybe."

Thanks A Latte isn't crowded when we walk in. I don't
see Caleb behind the counter, but I know he's on the
schedule until after the lunch rush. Maybe he's restocking
the shelves in the back. As I open the stockroom door, I see
Caleb through the safety window in the door. He's in the

back corner talking to someone; his back is to me, and he doesn't see or hear me entering. However, the girl he's cozied up with does. It's Ashlynn. *What the crap? Why is he always with her?*

Ashlynn notices my arrival and whispers something in Caleb's ear before rushing past me. Caleb's face is flushed, and guilt is written all over it. The scenario I just witnessed makes my gut clench. I didn't realize he and Ashlynn had gotten so close. I've got get out of here. Bursting back through the stockroom door, I grab Tammi's arm and pull her, causing her latte to spill.

"Leave it," I tell her and keep going.

"Tomorrow?" I hear Caleb call after me. "Wait!"

But I don't wait. I jump in the driver's seat, barely giving Tammi time to close her door before I tear out of the parking spot, and back down Kentworth Drive.

"Tomorrow, what's wrong?" Tammi struggles to lock her seatbelt. I guess I'm driving a little recklessly. "What happened?"

I don't answer her until we reach Ting Park, where I have no memories of Caleb I skid to a stop in the parking lot and realize tears are streaming down my cheeks. *What is wrong with me lately?*

"Did you know Caleb and Ashlynn are dating?"

"What? No," Tammi shakes her head adamantly. "They aren't dating. No way."

"I just saw them cuddled up in the stockroom together. When she saw me, she ran out. GUILTY."

"What did Caleb say?"

"Nothing, I took off."

"Tomorrow, you shouldn't have left." The admonishment in her tone was unmistakable.

"I panicked, okay?"

But why did I panic? Aren't Caleb and I just friends? He can date whomever he wishes, right? No, I don't want Caleb to date anybody else. I realize I've been too comfortable with the idea that Caleb will always be around for me and me only. I felt too damaged to admit my feelings for him. Now it's too late.

"Tomorrow, talk to Caleb."

My phone dings in my back pocket. It is Caleb's special ringtone.

Caleb: *Bug, what was that all about? Why did you run out of the shop like that?*

Tomorrow: *Uhm, I thought I heard someone calling me.*

Caleb: *Really? Wanna try that one again? I'll pretend I didn't read that one.*

Tomorrow: *I don't want to talk about it, okay?*

Caleb: *Did Troy do something?*

Tomorrow: *No, it wasn't anything like that. Let's forget it happened, okay?*

Caleb: *Okay, but I'll be by your house after work so we can forget it happened.*

"WELL, I guess I have no choice but to face the music now," I tell Tammi sheepishly.

"Why, what did he say?"

"He's coming over after his shift to talk."

"Good, let him explain. You guys are 'just friends' anyway, right?" she says in air quotes.

"Actually, I've had a thing for Caleb for years but never said anything. I didn't want to ruin our friendship. You know?" I expose myself to my best girlfriend for the first time. "Now, since Homecoming and what Troy did to me, there's no way Caleb would ever want anything to do with me other than be friends, so what's the point? Caleb is the greatest guy I've ever known. He has always been there for me, but I have taken advantage of that friendship and never thought he would find someone else to love. That's pretty selfish of me, isn't it?"

"Tomorrow, I have always felt you and Caleb were meant to be. Honestly, I think you are selling yourself and Caleb short. That isn't fair to either of you. Caleb loves you for who you are; whatever Troy did, only makes him love you more."

"That's exactly what Sierra said last week. She said I'm the same person in Christ, and anyone worthy of my love or loving me will recognize that."

"Your Stephen Minister is one smart cookie," Tammi leans over and hugs me. "You are as rare as gold."

Caleb's souped-up Mustang rumbles into the driveway. I can honestly say I'm not looking forward to this conversation. I don't want to hear about his relationship with Ashlynn, but I guess it's a necessary evil to clear the air between us. I don't want to lose Caleb as my best friend, and if that means stepping back because he has a girlfriend, then so be it.

Pacing the length of my room, I anxiously await his arrival. I feel like it has been an eternity since he pulled into the driveway, but I have yet to hear him enter the house or hear his footsteps on the hardwood stairs. *Where in the world can he be?*

I pull out my well-worn copy of *Pride and Prejudice*, killing time until we talk, but quickly put it away. I don't want him to walk in on me reading the book he bought me.

I think that would be counterproductive. Back in the night-stand it goes. I'm resigned to sitting at my desk in front of the window and tucking my trembling hands under my thighs.

I can hear it raining, but the forecast didn't call for rain today. Rays of sunbeams dance across my desktop through the window. *What the heck?* From my vantage point above the garage, I see Caleb washing Tater Bug. *What's he doing?* I thought we were supposed to be having an all-out war, not a carwash. Gripping my hoodie, I head downstairs and out the door.

"Caleb?" I yell loud enough for him to hear me over the earbuds stuck in both ears. "What are you doing?"

"Washing Tater Bug," he points to the new plate and gives me a toothy grin.

"I can see that, silly, but why?" The sun reflects off the shiny black paint on the hood, momentarily blinding me.

"I wanted to make you sweat a little before we address what happened at the coffee shop," he says, his smile broadening even wider. "I know how impatient you are."

"I thought we were going to forget it?" Wishful thinking on my part.

"Nope." He points the hose at me, forcing me to take cover behind the trash cans.

"Caleb! Stop!" We both laugh, but he shows no mercy. "Caleb!" Water arcs over the cans, drenching me, hoodie and all.

"Just trying to cool off that redhead temper of yours." He sprays me again.

"I don't have a redhead temper," I yell and charge him, determined to get the hose to retaliate in full force. Before I get close enough to grab the hose, he lurches in my direction and grabs me around the waist, spinning me around. He has my arms pinned at my sides and pulls me to him.

"No temper, huh?" His low and husky laugh makes my stomach tingle. Our lips are close enough to kiss, and for a second, I think we might. That is, until Today and Troy pull into the driveway behind Tater Bug, and the spell is broken.

15

"Aren't you two too cute," Troy says, sneering sarcastically as he gets out of his truck.

"What are you doing here?" Caleb moves slightly, blocking me from Troy's line of sight.

"I live here for seventy-two more days," Today says haughtily to Caleb, not acknowledging my presence. Her words sting my heart. Yes, she's counting the days until she can leave. I'm counting the days, praying for a miracle that she stays.

"That long, huh?" Caleb huffs. Today curls a lip at Caleb, disgusted that she's even interacting with us.

"I'll be right back, babe." She kisses Troy and heads into the house through the garage.

"So, Tomorrow, when will you come to see the new pad?" he asks, leaning against my car and crossing his ankles. "My folks remodeled the pool house into a fantastic apartment, especially the bedroom." He winks at me.

Caleb pushes Troy off my car. "Get away from her car," he demands. "And she has no interest in where you and Today are playing house."

I stand there, dripping wet, biting my thumbnail. I can't speak, but inwardly, I thank God that Caleb is here to stand in my steed. He's my hero.

"We're having a private conversation, and you are not invited to participate. So, get out of here," Caleb demands.

"I'm here with my wife. I'll leave when she's ready." Troy puffs out his chest, trying to be intimidating. Does he not know Caleb has a black belt in karate and can kick his ass anytime, anywhere? If I were Troy, I wouldn't push Caleb. But then again, I would love to see Caleb kick him to the curb.

Caleb laughs at Troy's response. "Your wife, what a joke." I'm sure a fight is about to break out in my driveway.

"Ready, babe?" Today emerges from the house just in time to see the standoff. "What's going on?"

"Nothing," Troy glares at Caleb. "Absolutely nothing. Let's go." He gets in the truck and slams the door.

Today glares at me as if I had something to do with the confrontation between the boys. If she hadn't come out, Troy would have gotten his butt kicked. To say Caleb hates Troy is the understatement of the century. Troy backs out of the driveway, throws the truck in drive, and squeals his tires as they leave the house. What a child, I think.

"I hate that guy," Caleb says, echoing my earlier thought. "I don't understand why you won't tell Today what an ass he is and what he tried to do you last fall." His frustration is evident in his voice.

"At this point, what good will it do? Besides, she believes his lie and thinks I want Troy." The thought turns my stomach. "She won't believe me; besides, they're married now. For the life of me, I don't understand why they got married. I mean, he can't really love her, right, if he tried to seduce me?" How many times have I recited these same thoughts and questions in my mind since last October? There are no answers, only more questions.

"I don't know Tater. I hate what he has done to you."

"Yeah, well, I'm freezing. I'm going to change out of these wet clothes. You should do the same."

"Okay, that's a good idea." Surprisingly, he agrees to go home. "But we still have to talk about earlier. I'll be back in about twenty minutes."

Shoot, he remembered.

"Fine," I retort and head to my bedroom. I'm so cold that my teeth are chattering. Either it's the wet clothes or the adrenaline pumping through my veins from seeing my sister with Troy. I'm not sure which. I don't want to have this conversation with Caleb. I don't think I can handle hearing that he and Ashlynn are becoming an item. Can't I live in my perfect little world where he stays single forever since I can't have him? I don't think that's too much to ask. Is it?

Fifteen minutes later, I hear a knock at my door as I dry off after a hot shower. Caleb said twenty minutes, not fifteen. I twist my hair in a towel and wrap up in my bathrobe. He could have given me five more minutes to get dressed. Geez, boys! Caleb is so impatient.

"Coming," I yell from the bathroom. I patter across the carpet, barefoot, and swing open the door. "You said twenty min—"

Instead of Caleb being the one at my bedroom door, it's Bree. Her face is blotchy, and dried tears are evident on her cheeks. She's the last person I expected to show up at my house. She's visibly upset, but I can't imagine why for the life of me.

"Bree, what are you doing here? What's wrong?" I'm stunned to see her. I don't think I've ever seen Bree cry in all the years we've been friends. She always seems so composed and in control of her life and destiny. Instead of answering my questions, she falls into me, apparently needing the comfort of a friend. I wrap her in a warm embrace and guide her into my room. Wrapping a blanket around her shoulders, we sit side by side on the window seat, holding hands.

"Bree, what's wrong?" I've never seen her so distraught.. "What happened?" I have to get some answers, so I know how to help her. My heart is breaking, and I don't even know why. I can't stand to see my friend so upset.

"I'm sorry I barged in without letting you know I was coming. I didn't know where else to go." She sniffs, and tears begin rolling down her face again. I grab a box of tissues for her from my nightstand before texting Caleb, telling him not to come over right now. We'll have to talk later.

"It's ok, Bree," I reassure her lovingly, "What's wrong?"

"I think I'm pregnant."

"Oh, goodness, Bree." I stand there, mouth agape, speechless.

"Yeah, that was kind of my reaction, too." She sniffles into the tissue again. "I can't believe this happened. I don't know what to do."

"Who is the father?" I hesitantly ask. He should be a part of this conversation—okay, maybe not *this* conversation, but involved in a discussion with Bree.

"It's no one you know." She looks away. Shame is written all over her face. "Besides, he won't want anything to do with the baby."

"How can you be so sure, Bree? Does he even know you're pregnant?" *Why do the guys think it's an option to help raise their child?*

"No, he doesn't know, and I won't tell him," Bree articulates firmly.

"Well, we can discuss that later. We need to make you a doctor's appointment with an OB/GYN." I grab my phone and start typing in a Google search.

"Not one in Holly Springs. Look in Apex or Garner. I don't want anyone in town to know I'm pregnant."

"Okay, but eventually, you won't be able to hide the pregnancy." I pray she isn't considering the alternative. Abortion is never the answer. I can understand her not being able to raise a child on her own, but there are too many couples that can't have children that would love to adopt her baby. Secretly, I hope it's a girl.

"Yeah." Bree is non-committal, which causes some worry.

"There are a few in Cary that are part of Wake Forest hospital," I say, as I read off a list of doctors. "Cary is only about twenty miles away. Is that far enough?"

"That's good. Are there any female doctors? I'd feel more comfortable with a woman."

"I don't blame you," I agree wholeheartedly. Reading a list of female doctors in Cary, I wonder how people ever found any information without the Internet. Mom says they used a phone book. I can't imagine.

Bree picks a name from the list I read and calls to make an appointment. They can't see her until next week, but she accepts the appointment anyway. I don't know if she's in a hurry to see the doctor and get the first appointment over, or if she wants to avoid it as long as possible. I don't know how I would feel in her situation. Other than being scared out of my mind.

"What am I going to tell Mom and Dad?" Bree says. I can see the fear and shame wash across her face. Bree and I aren't as close as Tammi and I are, and it's somewhat surprising that she came to me, but I'm glad she did. I want to help her, but I'm not sure that I can, other than being here for support. I assume that's what she needs most at this point.

"You don't need to tell them anything yet," I offer. "If they ask, tell them you decided it was time to get established with a gynecologist. We'll graduate soon and be on our own, so it makes sense, right?"

"Yeah, makes sense," she agrees.

"So, uhm..." I want details, but I'm not sure she will give them. I ask anyway. "How late are you, anyway?"

"Two weeks."

"Okay, and the test was positive?" I feel like a dweeb asking such an obvious question, but I'm new at this.

"I didn't take a test, but I have all the symptoms." Bree curls her legs under her as she sits on my bed and hugs Olaf to her chest. She looks like a little girl, not a mother-to-be. "Other than my period being so late, I'm nauseous all the time, moody, and extremely tired. I could sleep for twenty-four-hour stretches." A tear trails down her cheek. My heart breaks for her all over again. "All the signs are there."

"Sounds like it to me," I agree.

"Will you go with me next week?"

"Of course I will," I reassure her. "For now, let's go get some ice cream."

Bree and I sit on a bench outside Mama Bird's Ice Cream. I chow down on two scoops of blue Cookie Monster ice cream, and Bree has a cone of cotton candy. Mama Bird's makes the absolute best ice cream in Holly Springs. Their flavors are homemade and rotate, so it's always a surprise coming here.

"I love it when they make Cookie Monster ice cream," I say between bites. "I might have to go back in for another scoop." Yes, it's that good.

"I've never had it," Bree admits. "What's in it?"

"Oh my gosh, it's vanilla ice cream with chunks of chocolate chip, snickerdoodle, cookie dough, and Oreos. It's the bomb!"

"Morrow, you're drooling, eat up." She hands me a wad of napkins, and we giggle. "I had a feeling we'd need these."

After enjoying our ice cream at Mama Bird's, we returned to my house, discussing baby names the entire way. Dreaming up unique names like Mercedes for a girl and Dallas for a boy was fun, but I don't think Bree's heart was in it. I can't blame her, though. Her future is uncertain and scary. I wonder who the father is. She already shut that conversation down earlier, so I won't ask her again, but a nagging thought keeps running through my mind. Troy had Bree's number in his back pocket that day at Thanks A Latte. I hope that piece of paper and Bree's pregnancy aren't connected. They can't be—he's married to my sister. I'm being paranoid, that's all. Still, my stomach churns. I hope it's just too much ice cream.

"Bree, can I ask you a question?" I inquire without looking at her.

"That is a question," she says and smirks mischievously. It's good to see her smile.

"True," I chuckle in agreement. "But seriously, a couple of weeks ago, Troy and Today were in Thanks A Latte, and a piece of paper dropped out of Troy's back pocket when he put his wallet away. It had your number on it." I inhale deeply and watch her reaction out of the corner of my eye. She stiffens and takes a deep breath, but doesn't seem to relax. "I thought that was odd. I didn't know you were that close with him."

"Oh, that, yeah. We were working on a group project in world history, and we all exchanged numbers." Her words are so rushed that I can barely make sense of them. "I wondered why I had to give it to him twice." She laughs nervously, but her explanation makes some sense or is at least feasible.

The moment Bree backs out of the driveway, my phone dings with a text message from Caleb. He must have been watching to see when she left. I jump out of the fire into the frying pan. He wants to come over. I hoped to avoid the Ashlynn conversation, but today wasn't my lucky day.

Caleb: *Meet me at Veteran's Park at the workout station.*

Sighing heavily, I grab my hoodie and pull it over my head, put my hair up in a high ponytail, and grab my purse. This has been one exhausting day. I don't want to argue with Caleb, and I'm pretty sure I don't want to know the truth about him and Ashlynn. I hear his Mustang rumble to life next door and take off down the street. He expects me to follow him, but I take my time before leaving and stop for gas, before I end up stranded on the side of the road. I'm putting off this conversation as long as possible.

Twenty minutes later, as I pull into the Veteran's Park parking lot, I see Caleb's Mustang in front of the Little Free Library, the same one Tammi contributes to. I shut off Tater Bug's engine and watched four brown ducks approach Caleb's car. The ducks here expect to be fed, which I think is funny. I wonder if Caleb brought them any snacks, like peas or oats. We refuse to feed the ducks bread, which is bad for their stomachs. Thawed peas, lettuce, cracked corn, and uncooked oats are best for these little critters. We had a lecture in the eighth grade from a zoologist on the subject, so we never feed them bread. I didn't bring any goodies for the wildlife and am counting on Caleb to pick up the slack.

The ducks waddle their way to Caleb's car, and I watch to see if Caleb will open his door and feed them. He's so kind-hearted to people and animals; it's one of the things I love the most about him. The driver's side door doesn't open, which surprises me. What's he doing? The ducks are always a priority. Peering closer through the dark-tinted windows, I realize he isn't in his car alone. What the crap? He tells me to be here, but he's with someone else?

Just before I open my door and march to his car, I realize who's in the car with him. It's Ashlynn. Talk about rubbing it in my face! I don't need to hear any of his excuses now. I've seen all I need to see. I fire up the engine in my Beetle and take off.

Oh, God, how stupid can I be?

16

As I speed away from Veteran's Park, my cellphone buzzes with a text from Caleb.

Caleb: *Please, Morrow, come back. Let me explain.*

I ignore the text and keep driving. I meander the streets of Holly Springs aimlessly until I find myself outside Troy's parent's house. I assume Today is in their "apartment pool house" in the home's backyard. Instinctively, I want to talk to my sister about Caleb and Ashlynn. She's always been my go-to person when I have a problem. Realizing that she isn't the same person anymore and hates me for false reasons, I leave with tears in my eyes. *God, my life is falling apart around me. I need you*, I think.

Since I can't talk to Today, I head to Tammi's. I already know what she's going to tell me. She'll give me a speech about how Caleb loves me, and there must be another explanation, and that I'm overreacting. After seeing how Ashlynn flirts with Caleb at school, seeing them together at Thanks A Latte, and then today she was in his car when he knew I was meeting him, I don't see how I'm overreacting. Heck, he told me to meet him there!

Tammi lives in the Bridgeberry neighborhood of Holly Springs. I adore her neighborhood. It's a relatively new community, but the rolling hills and tree-filled lots are beautiful. I especially love the butterfly garden, which opens in the spring. Tammi is lucky to live in such a luxurious neighborhood. Mind you, I've never been jealous of where she lives, but I do love to visit. She lives on a corner lot with a tree-lined driveway, a swimming pool, and a perfectly manicured lawn. Her mom is all about curb appeal. Instead of driving up to her house, I keep going. I don't feel like a lecture from her today, and believe me, she can lecture when she thinks she's right about something. However, I must admit, she's usually right about her hunches. I guess I don't want her to be right about Caleb. I mean, I do, but right now, I don't believe her hunch. I've seen too much between Caleb and Ashlynn to believe otherwise.

Shooting off a quick text to Sierra asking for prayer, I leave Bridgeberry and head toward home. I have nowhere else to go. Instead of Sierra telling me she would pray for me, she suggested we meet for coffee, and I said I was good with that. I turn Tater Bug toward Garner to meet her at Jitter Bean again. Sierra is becoming more than a Stephen Minister; she's becoming a friend.

Twenty-five minutes later, while pulling in front of Jitter Bean, I get a text from Troy. The text contains a picture of Caleb and Ashlynn together at Thanks A Latte in the stockroom. How in the world did he take this picture? He's like the Secret Service or something. The text reads:

Troy: *Boy toy seems to have a new bombshell.*

I can't take much more drama in my life, so instead of stooping to Troy's level and taking the bait, I delete the text and enter the coffee shop to wait for Sierra. Jitter Bean is warm and cozy, filled with brown overstuffed leather chairs, mahogany woodwork, floor-to-ceiling bookshelves, and tables tucked into corners for private conversations. I place my order and select one of the secluded tables to wait for Sierra.

I don't have to wait long for Sierra to arrive. She's a pretty girl with short, wavy brown hair, trendy large-frame glasses, blue eyes, healthy curves, and dimples. She is what most would call 'cute'. I don't care for the word, 'cute'; it's like 'fine'. It's so non-committal. Anyway, Sierra gets green tea and a scone before finding me hiding in the corner.

"Hey, Tomorrow," Sierra says and leans over to kiss me on the cheek. "Are you okay? I got here as fast as I could."

"Overwhelmed," I admit honestly. "So many things are going wrong in my life that I sort of snapped."

"I want to hear all about it, but first, let me pray for our time together." She prays for peace, patience, understanding, and clear direction. I feel better that she brought God into our conversation. I hope he heard her. I need some clarity and direction in my life. Everything has been turned upside down, and I feel like I'm cracking under the pressure. Caleb and Ashlynn are the straw that broke the camel's back.

"Okay, so tell me, what has changed since we last spoke? I was surprised to get your text," she says.

"I'm sorry," I tell her sheepishly. "I didn't mean to scare you. I just don't know what to do or where to turn. Everything is going wrong."

"Okay, start from the beginning and tell me what happened." Sierra leans forward on her elbows and cocks her head to one side. She looks like a puppy when you talk to them, and they lift an ear to try to understand, but have a vacant stare. They're as cute as can be, but not very useful. Sierra is a good listener, unlike the puppy kind.

"Well, Tammi and I went to Thanks A Latte this morning. I knew Caleb was working, and I wanted to show him the new license plate my parents gave me for my car. It says my nickname, 'TATERBUG. ' I knew Caleb suggested it, so I wanted to thank him. When we arrived, I saw him and Ashlynn in the back corner of the stockroom, all cozy-like, so I left. Caleb came over after his shift to talk, but he started washing my car instead of coming into the house. I went outside, and we had fun joking and whatnot, but before we could talk, Today and Troy showed up, which is never a good scene. Anyway, they were only there for a few minutes and left. I went inside to change out of my wet clothes, and Caleb went to do the same at his house, so we could eventually have 'the talk' about the stockroom. But, before Caleb could come over, Bree showed up at my house. We're close, but not that close, and I was surprised she just showed up. Anyway, she told me she was pregnant, and the father was not in the picture. She asked me to go to the doctor with her next week. Of course, I said yes. After she left, Caleb texted me, asking me to meet him at Veteran's Park to talk. When I get there, he's with Ashlynn again! I took off and mindlessly drove to see Today. Habit, I guess. Realizing she wouldn't even talk to me, everything sort of crashed in on me. That's when I texted you." Wow, I said all of that in one fell swoop. I'm not even sure I took a breath.

"Wait," Sierra pauses and contemplates all the trash I just spewed out. "All this happened *today*?"

"Yup."

"No wonder you are tied in knots, girl."

"I know, right?"

"Let me get this straight. You saw Caleb with Ashlynn twice today."

"Right. At Thanks A Latte and Veteran's Park."

"Were they hugging, kissing, anything of the sort?"

"Uhm, no. Not that I saw." I know where this line of questioning is headed. I had asked myself the same questions while waiting for Sierra to arrive.

"And Caleb asked you several times to meet so he could explain?"

"Yeah, but probably to explain they're an item now."

"Do you know that or assume it?"

"Assuming, I guess." I'm losing my resolve the more she rationalizes.

"You know what they say about assuming, right?" She smirks mischievously. "You could be right about Caleb and Ashlynn, although I have a hunch there's more to the story than you're aware of. You need to let Caleb explain the situation entirely before you fill in the blanks with your own version. You would want him to do the same if the roles were reversed, wouldn't you?"

"Yeah, I would. But I saw—"

"We all know looks can be deceiving," Sierra says, cutting me off. "What we observe can sometimes be more of a preconceived notion rather than reality. I can't see Caleb trying so hard to explain if he doesn't feel that somewhere, there are misunderstandings. Granted, I don't know Caleb personally, but based on the way you describe him, that's what my heart is telling me." She reaches over and squeezes my hand reassuringly. "Give Caleb a chance to explain. If you're right, at least you can deal with the truth instead of making assumptions. If you're wrong, you end up with egg on your face."

"Very funny, Sierra." I can't keep the sarcasm from my

voice. She's right, though. I didn't give Caleb a chance to explain. What if I'm jumping to conclusions? I don't know what to think. I do know that I wouldn't blame him for dating Ashlynn. I'm not girlfriend material.

"Have you told Caleb how you feel about him?" she asks me sincerely. "Knowing what you have been through with Troy, I would venture to guess you've either given him mixed signals or none at all."

"I can't really give him signals since I don't know exactly how I feel. I mean, he's my best friend. As many times as my friends have told me that Caleb loves me, I never thought much of it. Well, until Ashlynn came along." I rest my chin in my hands, elbows on the table, and sigh. "And I don't think Caleb would want anything to do with me now after Troy touched me in places..." I trailed off, not wanting to relive the assault.

"First, what Troy did does not change who or what you are. Thank God he didn't rape you, but he did enough to cause you to feel ashamed of yourself. That isn't fair. You did nothing wrong; you are the victim, and now what he did is affecting all areas of your life. Second, if Caleb loves you like your friends say he does, he doesn't think any less of who you are. Love is unconditional, Tomorrow. Love is patient and kind. Caleb hasn't left you or abandoned your friendship since the incident, has he?"

"No, he's become even *more* protective over me."

"From what you've told me, he's a good guy. You need to stop feeling shame over someone else's actions. In this case, Troy's actions." Sierra reached across the table and squeezed my hand gently. "You are not to blame."

"But I feel so stupid. I feel like I betrayed my sister. I feel like I should have been able to fight him off. I shouldn't have gotten in the truck with him. I shouldn't have been so gullible." Staring into my cup, I absently stir the foam until it's all but disappeared.

"Why should you feel stupid? He was practically a part of your family. He and your sister have been together for a long time. You trusted him. The fault is his, not yours. You need to stop blaming yourself."

I know Sierra is right but knowing in my head is different from knowing in my heart. I'm tired of feeling shame and guilt. I'm also tired of being blamed for all the drama when the fault is his. He attacked me, not the other way around, but I don't have a clue as to how to rectify the situation. Everything is so twisted when it comes to Today and Troy. It's easier to do nothing and suffer.

17

The next morning, I take my time getting out of bed and getting myself ready for school. I don't want to face Caleb. I spent last night tossing and turning, trying to figure out what I would say to him. I have several options, depending on what he tells me about him and Ashlynn. If I'm wrong about the two of them, and they aren't dating, I don't think I'm ready to tell him I have feelings for him. If he tells me they are dating, it'll take everything in me not to fall apart on the spot.

When I finally emerge from my bedroom, Mom is the only one in the kitchen. She looks at her watch and frowns. "Running a little late this morning?" *Why do moms ask rhetorical questions?* I think to myself.

"I didn't sleep well," I respond anyway.

"Are you feeling okay, honey?" She switches into nurse mode.

"I'm fine. It's just a big test today," I lie.

"I'm sure you'll do fine, dear."

"Yeah, thanks," I say, grabbing a cup of coffee and a Pop-

Tart from the cupboard before heading out the door. "I gotta go, so I can make my first class. Love you."

"I love you too, sweetie. Good luck!" Mom calls as I close the kitchen door behind me.

I do a pretty good job of avoiding Caleb all day. I rush from class to class, so I won't run into him in the halls, hide out in a secluded corner of the library at lunch, and wait until the last possible moment before entering French class, sitting down just as the bell rings. However, not five minutes into class, he slips me a note written in French.

Bien essayé, Tater Tot. Je te retrouverai sur le parking après les cours. This translates to *Nice try, Tater Tot. I will meet you in the parking lot after class.*

I still haven't decided what I'll say to him. I guess I'll find out when the time comes—forty-three minutes from now.

Waiting on Caleb after school feels like I'm standing on the receiving end of a firing squad, and I think I'm going to throw up. Why did I agree to meet him? I should have stayed home from school today and convinced my parents to send me to live with my aunt and uncle in Wyoming. That way, I'll never face Caleb and this life-changing discussion. I can't tell him how I feel, and I also can't face him dating Ashlynn. I'm facing a no-win conversation. Beads of sweat appear on my forehead, my hands tremble, my stomach churns, and my knees knock. I thought that only happened in books, but here I am, freaking out. I'm two seconds away from chickening out when I see Caleb crossing the parking lot toward me—with Ashlynn in tow.

"Uhm, hi guys?" I greet them in a questioning tone, staring down Caleb. I thought this was going to be a private conversation, but instead, Caleb brings his new girlfriend. What's the point of this conversation? Is he trying to rub it in my face or to get me over the shock of seeing them locked arm-in-arm around the school from now on? Either way, I think it's pretty crappy of him. I thought we were better friends than that.

"Hi, Tomorrow," Ashlynn rushes at me and wraps me in a big hug. *Wow, this is awkward*, I think. I stiff-arm hug her back, wide-eyed, glaring at Caleb, trying to convey, *what the crap?* Which, of course, he misses completely.

"Hi, Ashlynn," I murmur and step back a few feet, bouncing my gaze between the two of them.

"Hey, Tater," Caleb addresses me. That's big of him. At least he still knows my name. My thought-voice can be pretty sarcastic sometimes. "I ran into Ashlynn on my way out. I told her I was headed to meet you, and she asked to tag along because she wanted to ask you something."

"Oh, okay." Now I feel like a heel.

"You know Austin Sheldon, right?" she asks and blushes. Now, I'm thoroughly confused. If she's with Caleb, why is she asking about Austin? God help me, this girl is so blonde.

"Yeah, I know him."

"Well, Caleb told me the other day that Austin joined Caleb's karate class, and he asked Caleb about me." She squeals like a little girl, bouncing on her toes and clasping her hands together. Her face even blushes when she mentions Austin's name. She looks sort of cute and innocent as she rattles on and on about Austin, and here I thought Ashlynn was this confident, beauty queen type of girl. "As it turns out, according to Caleb, next week is Austin's birthday. I was thinking we—well, me— could throw him a surprise birthday party. Maybe then he'll actually talk to me. So, anyway, I was wondering if you would come?"

"Oh." This isn't the line of conversation I was expecting. I can't say that I'm not pleased, though. Ashlynn is all gaga over Austin, not Caleb. Glancing at Caleb, he winks at me and smirks. I'm going to punch him in the gut for that later. "Of course, I will. I've known Austin since elementary school. Just send me the details. Okay?"

"That's great! I've been bombarding Caleb every time I see him, but guys are only so helpful." Ashlynn giggles, and I nod in agreement. "Oh, and could you extend an invitation to your sister and Troy once I have the time and place worked out? I would love for them to come, too."

I blanch at the mention of my sister and her "husband."

"I think the invitation would be better coming directly from you, Ashlynn," Caleb says quickly. As usual, Caleb jumps to my rescue.

"Yeah, you're probably right. Okay, I'm out." She waves and turns to leave. "I'll send you the info later this week, Tomorrow. Bye, guys." With that, she trots across the parking lot.

"So, I think my work here is done, and I didn't even have to say a word," Caleb says smugly.

"Yeah, but..." I start to defend myself.

"Nope, no buts. You jumped to conclusions, not that I expected any less, but you were wrong."

"I see that now." I touch his arm lightly, feeling like a fool. "I'm so sorry."

"Bah, no problem," Caleb chuckles and embraces me in a heartfelt hug. "I kind of like seeing you jealous. That tells me I have a chance."

"A chance with what?" My stomach lurches and ties in knots.

"You'll see," Caleb winks and opens my car door. "Don't you have a shift this afternoon?"

"I do," I confirm, looking away before speaking again. "Thank you."

"For reminding you to go to work?" I hear his jovial tone, and he winks when I look up at him.

"Yeah, exactly." I punch him in the arm.

"You're welcome, Tater. We're good now, right?"

"We're good." It's a rare friend with whom you can have an entire conversation to clear the air without speaking a word. Caleb and I are that kind of friends.

"I love spring," I tell my friends as we sit on the quad at lunchtime, soaking up the warm breeze and sunshine. "I hate being cooped up in the house all winter and how everything looks dead. But look at it now. The trees are budding, the flowers are blooming, and the grass is sprouting."

"Aren't you just Walt Whitman today?" Caleb teases, but I ignore him and keep munching my Oreo cookies. "Give me one of those," he says. I know they're his favorite.

"Nope, these are all mine. Get your own," I say, pulling the baggie from his reach. I don't share my Oreos.

"Ah, Tater Tot, come on. Just one," he lowers his eyelids in a pitiful puppy dog way. "Please?"

"Oh, okay, but just one." I carefully select one of the icing-filled cookies and hand it to him. "But just this one."

"Thanks, Tomorrow!" he exclaims and pops the entire cookie in his mouth and crunches it between his teeth. His face turns a putrid shade of green as realization dawns on him. He spits the cookie on the ground and chugs a drink of his Coke. "Oh my god, what the hell, Morrow?"

Tammi and I are doubled over with laughter at his reaction. "April's Fools!" I scream when I catch my breath. "I replaced the filling with toothpaste!" More laughter ensues from my friends and I. My sides ache from laughing so hard at Caleb's expense. I love it.

"That's classic, Tomorrow," Jeremy agrees, laughing hardily. "I'll have to pull that one on my little brother." Bree and Carly are laughing, too. It isn't easy to get a prank over on Caleb, but this one worked. I laugh for a full five minutes before my breathing returns to normal.

"You know what this means, don't you, Morrow?" Caleb mocks in all seriousness.

"That you don't have to brush your teeth after lunch?" I can't help but snicker at my own joke.

"No, it means revenge," he says, cackling maniacally.

The warning bell rings, signaling the end of our lunch period. I hate going back into the building, but at least the day is half over. Turning to Bree, I whisper, "I'll meet you in the parking lot after school. I'll drive."

She doesn't respond but nods her head in agreement. I can see the nervousness on her face. Today is her first doctor's appointment with the OB/GYN for the baby. I'm nervous for her, but I promised I would be by her side, and I always keep my word.

As we go our separate ways to class, I give Caleb one last glance. With a sinister gleam in his eye, he nods and gives a two-finger salute. I can't help but feel he's going to do something devious in retaliation for the Oreo toothpaste prank. This should be good...or not. Horrific scenarios run through my mind, and I think of the revenge he'll inflict upon me. Caleb is quite the crafty one.

Suspiciously, Caleb is absent from French today, which doesn't bode well for me. I do my best to concentrate on

Mrs. James, as she has various students conjugate verbs. Please, Lord, don't let her call on me, I think.

The final bell of the day rings, signaling our freedom. I grab my purse and backpack, make a quick stop at my locker, and head for the door. Bree is waiting for me as I emerge from the building, so we can get to her appointment in Garner. A crowd of students is gathered in the parking lot, laughing at something I can't see. We maneuver our way through the crowd to get to Tater Bug, and then, it all makes sense.

My mouth hangs wide open as I stare at my baby Beetle. Caleb has completely encompassed her, headlights to tailpipe, in plastic wrap. Top to bottom, side to side, front to back, with a box of Oreo cookies and a tube of Crest resting on the roof.

O-M-G!

Bree bursts out laughing, along with the rest of the students, but all I can do is stare in disbelief. Now I know why he skipped class today. That little bugger wasn't kidding when he said he would get revenge.

"We all know the culprit behind this beautiful wrap job," Bree comments. "I have to admit, he's creative and works fast!"

"Ya think?"

"Can I have a cookie?" I hear Caleb call from the back of the crowd. The students between us move aside like Moses parting the Red Sea, allowing Caleb to approach his master-piece. "I didn't eat much lunch. For some unknown reason, everything tasted like mint."

I can't help but laugh at him. Caleb is crazy, quick-witted, and good-humored. I have to give him kudos for the quick retaliation.

"Sure, after you help me unwrap this mess, so I can get to a doctor's appointment."

"Oh, that's easy enough," he says and whips out his pocketknife. Starting at the rear, he slices the plastic wrap in one long swipe from tail to front, and it peels like a banana. "Easy peasy," he says, grinning like a monkey and grabbing the Oreos.

"Hey, you asked for one Oreo!" I stomp my foot in mock anger.

"Yeah, one box!" He takes off toward his Mustang, leaving laughter in his wake.

"You can't help but love that guy," Bree says.

"Yeah, gotta love him," I admit.

∾

"I DON'T WANT to go in," Bree whines as we pull into the OB/GYN's office parking lot.

"I know it's scary, but the baby needs a doctor to watch over her."

"Her, huh?" Bree giggles, her anxiety bubbling over. "You think it's a girl?"

"Well, Auntie Morrow can hope."

"I guess I can't put this off any longer." She inhales deeply, opens the passenger side door, and I see her hands trembling. My heart goes out to her. I can't imagine being in her position. But I'm a virgin, so no worries there.

"I'll be right here, waiting." I hope I sound reassuring. "Good luck."

"Thanks," Bree smiles weakly and closes the door behind her.

I watch her as she makes her way to the doctor's office entrance. I feel sorry for her because I can't imagine becoming a mother at eighteen years old and unmarried. I would be scared crapless. Her life is just beginning, but I have no doubt she'll be a great mom and give that baby a wonderful life filled with love, even if the father isn't in the picture. I can't help but wonder who he is. Do I know him? Is he from Holly Springs? I haven't known Bree to really date anyone our entire senior year, which, come to think of it, is odd. Don't cheerleaders always have a boyfriend on the football team? Life is full of unanswered questions.

I spend about thirty minutes browsing websites listing popular baby names, unusual baby names, quirky baby names, and finally, historic names before switching to shopping. I open the Amazon app on my phone and start browsing baby clothes. Since the baby's gender is unknown right now, I create "favorite lists" on my account—one for a baby girl and one for a baby boy—and start saving cute clothes, toys, bottles, pacifiers, bedding, and rattles to the lists. Just as I'm about to drop a Noah's Ark plush stuffed animal play set onto my list, Bree yanks the door open and scares the life out of me. I didn't see her coming out of the office.

"Oh my goodness, Bree," I exclaim. "That was fast."

Bree doesn't acknowledge me or my comment. She merely sits in the passenger seat, staring through the windshield, not saying a word. She looks a little pale leaving me totally clueless as to what she's feeling or thinking. I'm not sure what to say, but I have to say something, right?

"Uhm, Bree. What did the doctor say? Did they figure out your due date? When is your next appointment?" I have so many questions, and I need answers.

Slowly, she turns to me, as a tear trickles down her cheek.

"I'm not pregnant," she states, matter-of-factly.

"Wait, what? How can that be? The test you took was wrong?"

"I never took a test. All the signs and symptoms were there. I knew I was pregnant."

'You never took a test??"

"No, I didn't. I just assumed I was pregnant." Her gaze never leaves the floorboard of my car. She doesn't look at me as she continues with her explanation. "The timing was right. I was sick all the time, tired, and had a missed period. All signs that pointed toward me being pregnant with his child." Bree looks sad, as though she's sorry the pregnancy is false.

"Uhm, okay," I say as I try to regroup and delete the favorites lists from my phone. "So, what did the doctor say?"

"He said I have a severe kidney infection and prescribed antibiotics."

"You don't seem happy about this." I'm totally confused.

"I already loved this baby, ya know?" She twists a tissue in her hands. I feel so bad for her.

"I understand that. I was picking out clothes and baby names."

"Let me get over the shock," she says, as she chuckles at my admission. "And I have no doubt that relief will hit me."

We sit in silence for a few minutes, digesting the news. Before long, Bree starts to laugh. I wasn't expecting laughter to fill the small space of my car, but it does. I don't know if she has just lost her mind or if the relief just dawned on her. Either way, it's good to hear her laugh after all the stress she's been under.

"Bree?"

"Thank God I won't have to tell my parents I'm pregnant and my cheerleading uniform will still fit." We both laugh at her absurd thought process, and I can't help but feel her relief. A little sadness still lingers in her voice, but peace overshadows it.

"Let's head back to Holly Springs and grab an ice cream at Mama Bird's to celebrate."

"Good idea," Bree agrees. I back Tater Bug out of her parking space and turn toward home.

Crisis averted!

18

Group Text Recipients:
        Carly, Wesley, Tammi, Jeremy,
        Caleb, Tomorrow, Troy, Today,
Marcus, Cindy, Jacob, Kyle,
Misti, Allison, Jason, Darrell,
Josh, Soran, Amy, Alex
Shhhh!
It's a surprise birthday cookout!
Come join the fun!

WHEN: April 17th @ 1 p.m.
    Where: Ting Park
    Why: Austin's 18th Birthday
    What's provided:
    Hamburgers & hot dogs
    Cake & ice Cream
    Sodas & tea
    Frisbee golf & cornhole
    RSVP to Ashlynn by the 15th

"I don't know half of the people Ashlynn invited to Austin's cookout," I tell Caleb the day before the party. "But it'll be a beautiful day for it—sunny and clear." After reading Caleb the next day's forecast, I slide my phone into my back pocket and recline in the patio chair on the deck overlooking our pool. Caleb and I have spent thousands of hours on this deck, in the pool, or tossing a baseball in the backyard. His property adjoins ours, and there's a gap in the bushes where we always cross into each other's yard. It's more convenient that way. Since his mom passed away, he's become part of our family, and I couldn't be happier.

"Marcus, Jacob, Kyle, and Darrell are on the karate team; I don't know the rest. Must be people from school," Caleb explains. "I wonder if your sister and Buttmunch are going?" He voices the question I've been wondering for days. I hope they don't show. Knowing Troy, he'll think a birthday party is beneath him.

"Whatcha got planned tonight, Tater?" Caleb doesn't look at me when he asks, which I find odd. He's asked me that same question a million times over the years. Instead of looking in my direction, he's cleaning under his fingernails with his pocketknife. Gross. Why do guys do that? My dad does it, too, especially after working in the garden or on one of our cars. As Mom calls it, Dad is always "tinkering" in the garage. Why can't they use soap like everyone else?

"Tammi and I are going to Wine & Design in Apex tonight. I'm so excited! I've never been before. Have you?"

"What the heck is Wine and Design?" Caleb scrunched his nose in the cutest gesture I've ever seen.

"It's a place where you sign up for a two-hour art class,

bring a friend, sip some wine, and create! They're all over the country, have you had your head in the sand, or what?" Excitement oozes from my pores. "Anyway, obviously, Tammi and I will be drinking non-alcoholic beverages, but still, it should be fun. We signed up for the "Paint Your Pet" class. Local artists guide you through how to paint the project step by step. I sent in a picture of Penelope, and if the painting turns out okay, I'm going to give it to Faith for her birthday."

"Take a breath, Sweet Tater, before you pass out," he says, teasing me. "I'm sure you guys will have fun, but I didn't know you could paint."

"Oh, well, I can't," I giggle and shrug my shoulders. "That's where the local artists come in."

"Good luck with that, Tater."

"Hey, why don't you come with us?" The idea hits me like a bolt from heaven. "It'll be fun."

"No, I think I'll skip this one," Caleb says, hanging his head a little and not looking at me. "Maybe some other time."

"Oh, I see how it is; you want me to be the guinea pig."

"Yeah, something like that." Caleb's voice is uncharacteristically low. He's usually vibrant, boisterous, and full of life. Getting up from his lounge chair, he grabs his keys off the side table and tucks them in his front pocket. "Have fun tonight, Tater Bug. See you later." Taking off, he runs through my backyard and disappears through the hedges that divide our properties. *That was a really weird conversation*, I think to myself. But then again, Caleb has his weird moments. Without giving it another thought, I grab our empty glasses of lemonade and head through the sliding glass door into the house. I need to get ready anyway, might as well start early.

"YOU'RE AN IDIOT," Tammi says, scolding me with a hint of amusement as we paint our canvases' backdrops. I've chosen to paint Penelope in a field of daisies on a spring day. Tammi is going to paint her dog, Joy, a black lab mix, paddling in the pool. Joy hated the water as a puppy; it would take them an hour for her to go out to potty in the rain. But now that she's older, she loves the water, and they had to put a fence around the pool to keep her out. Most people put fences around in-ground pools for the safety of little children, but not Tammi's family. They have to put a fence up to keep Joy dry. I think it's hilarious.

"Why am I an idiot?" I question. I don't understand why she's saying such a thing about her best friend. Well, I do, but I won't admit that to her.

"Caleb was going to ask you out, silly."

"No, he wasn't. He was just asking about my plans," I say, correcting her, although I purposefully left out the part where he was preoccupied with his fingernails and wouldn't look at me. Also, he did leave rather abruptly.

"Again, you're an idiot," she says, shaking her head. Then she turns back to her canvas and keeps painting the water in the pool.

"Why do you avoid Caleb's advances?" Tammi asks quietly into her canvas. "Is it because of that night?"

Is it that obvious that I avoid Caleb's attempts of asking me out? I'm very confused by my feelings of falling for Caleb and my shame over Troy seeing parts of my naked body. I still have nightmares about that night. I wish I had never told Caleb what happened. That way, I could bury my emotions and move on with my life. Maybe. Goodness, I thought I was moving past these feelings of guilt. Why do they keep surfacing? I don't know if I'll ever be whole again.

Placing my paintbrush in the jar of turpentine, I whisper, "Caleb deserves someone...better." The acrid smell of the turpentine stings my nostrils as I sniff back a tear. My hands start to tremble, so I shove them in the pocket of my paint apron before Tammi notices. Tonight was supposed to be a fun evening, not what it's quickly turning into, which is a night full of sadness and depression.

"Better?" Tammi asks, as she holds her brush inches from the canvas and then freezes.

Inhaling a deep breath, I turn to Tammi with tear-filled eyes. "I'm damaged goods, Tammi. Caleb deserves better." The confession is both confining and freeing. "You should probably tell Caleb I'm a lost cause. He should find someone better suited to a relationship. I'm not girlfriend material."

"Do you honestly believe Caleb thinks that about you? That's complete bull, if you ask me," she says and continues to paint Joy in the pool.

"Tammi, how can he not? I mean, Troy saw my breast and touched me; he tried to kiss me and groped me. My god, you don't understand." My emotions peak to a level they haven't reached in a long time. Tammi and I rarely fight, but I can't hold back. "I thought you would understand, but you have a solid, steady boyfriend in Jeremy, so how could you understand?" I rip off the apron, tossing it aside, and grab my belongings from under the table. I'm out of here. I only feel marginally bad for taking my frustration out on Tammi. But, dang, is she so shallow that she thinks I should be over the incident so soon? I mean, it's only been six months. I push through the glass doors of Wine & Design and face-plant right into Caleb's chest.

"Whoa, where's the fire?" Caleb wraps his arms around me, keeping me from falling.

"Oh, my God!" I scream. "What are you doing here, Caleb?" I can't believe I ran right into him. but then again, he always catches me when I fall.

"You invited me, remember?" He's so cute when the corner of his lip turns upward when he smirks. "What's wrong? Did Penelope turn out looking like a raccoon instead of a skunk?" Caleb chuckles at his own humor.

Taking a step back, I wipe under my eyes, in case any tears are still there. "Funny," I say, my voice flat, and I feel the absence where his arms had been wrapped around me just seconds ago.

"Oh, hey, Caleb," Tammi greets him as she pushes through the same door from which I had just emerged. "What are you doing here?"

"Tomorrow invited me, so she wouldn't be the only one here that can't paint." He chuckles and pulls me close to his side protectively.

She gives me a pointed look and hands me my canvas, wrapped in brown craft paper. "She did a great job, but we're finished. You missed the main event. But, if you guys want to go do something, I can go to Jeremy's." She winks in my direction, and I wanted to kill her right then and there.

"Let's go to The Blind Pelican. I'm in the mood for seafood." He looks directly at me when he asks.

"When are you not in the mood for seafood?" I ask sarcastically.

"Hey! I haven't had their amazing lobster and scallop pasta in at least a month." He rubs his belly like a genie. "I'm having withdrawals."

"You told me your dad took you to The Blind Pelican last weekend," I say, reminding him with scrunched eyebrows.

My left hand is on my hip, and my lip is turned up in one corner.

"Well, yeah." Caleb backpedals with reddening cheeks. "But I had shrimp and grits, not lobster and scallops."

"Why don't you two fight over the menu on the way, and I'll go get Jeremy and meet you there?" I can almost see the gears turning in Tammi's mind, and I know she's trying to make this into a double date. My suspicions are confirmed when she winks at me before strolling off in the opposite direction from Wine & Design.

"All right, Tater Tot, let's go. We'll probably have to wait for a table this late in the evening, so I want to get in line." Caleb grabs my hand and pulls me down the sidewalk toward his car. "I can smell the lobster now," he says, as he inhales deeply. "Can't you?"

"The only thing I can smell is the paint and turpentine on this canvas."

"You are such a buzzkill, you know that?" He flashes his dimple in my direction, causing my resolve to stay away from him to dissolve a fraction. "I'm going to have to see what I can do about that." That comment sends my stomach into knots. I can't deny the feelings I have for Caleb; it's acting upon them that's the issue.

As we approach his car, he presses a button on the key fob, making the car beep several times before the Mustang roars to life, stopping me in my tracks. I didn't expect that. "When did you get a remote start on the Stang?" He's always upgrading his baby with the newest gadgets. This one I'm jealous of. I wish my Tater Bug had a remote start for hot days, so it would be nice and cool inside after school. I hate getting in a hot car and the seats sticking to my back from sweat.

"Yesterday, actually." He beams with pride. "Dad had it

installed as an early graduation gift. I couldn't wait to show you."

"Is that why you drove over here to Apex?" It was all making sense now. He wanted to show off his car, not to see me. I feel like an idiot, just as Tammi called me earlier.

"That wasn't the only reason, Tomorrow." His voice is low and gentle. "I wanted to talk to you about something." He opens the passenger side door, allowing me to slide into the cool leather seats. This car is like a second home to me. I always feel safe and comfortable sitting beside Caleb in his car. But tonight, it's different. I have butterflies in my stomach, and I know if Caleb brings up the subject of us dating, I'll have to squash the idea like a cockroach on the kitchen floor. The thought breaks my heart, but I must spare him.

We ride in silence for the first five minutes of the trip back to Holly Springs. The silence is strained and awkward. From the corner of my eye, I can see him gripping the steering wheel so firmly that his knuckles turn white. The tension is unbearable, and one of us has to break it. Before I can come up with a safe topic for conversation, he speaks up.

"I hate this road." The sound of his voice startles me, but at least it shatters the silence. "People drive like it's an autobahn."

"Yeah, I'm glad I don't have to come this way very often," I agree.

"Anyway, I wanted to talk to you about prom."

"I'm not—" I say, trying to shoot this conversation down, but he interrupts me.

"I know you don't want to go. I know it brings up too many bad memories. And I know Today and Troy will be there. But Tater, I really want you to go, and I want you to go with me." He inhales deeply, as if it took everything in him to get all said before I freak out.

"Go stag together again?" The memories of Homecoming jump to the forefront of my consciousness. Oddly, they aren't the memories of Troy but the memories of the excitement of going with Caleb.

"No, Tomorrow, going as my date." He glances sideways to see my reaction, and I smile at him.

"Oh, Caleb, I—" *SCREECH!* Headlights blind me momentarily, beaming through Caleb's driver-side window. A thought flashed in my brain: *why are those headlights so close?* The sound of tires skidding on the pavement, metal twisting, and glass shattering fills my ears. My head is flung to the left, but my body and the car violently jerk to the right. Caleb is instantly on my side of the car, and I'm crushed against the passenger side door. His face is splattered with blood from the spray of glass as his side window shatters, and he's twisted at an unnatural angle. His Mustang is tossed like a Matchbox car across the intersection, and we're flung against a light pole. The car comes to a complete stop with a sudden jerk, but I can't move. I'm pinned between Caleb and the door, and he isn't moving. Blood and glass are everywhere. I try to open the door, but it's bent out of shape.

"Caleb," I whisper, but he doesn't respond.

"Caleb," I say louder, but there isn't any movement from him, whatsoever.

"Caleb!" I scream into the blackness of the car. "Caleb! No! No! No! No!" I panic, screaming his name over and over. "Caleb, please wake up! I love you, Caleb, I think I always have. Wake up, so we can go to prom. Please, wake up!" I hear sirens in the distance; I hope they are coming to save Caleb. God, please, I can't live with him. *Please save Caleb.* I plead this mantra in my head until I pass out. Not knowing if Caleb heard my confession. Not knowing if he is even alive.

A light shines in my eyes, pulling me from my unconsciousness. "She's alive," a deep male voice shouts above my head. "Get a paramedic over here as soon as the ambulance arrives!"

"Did you see what happened?" I hear another male voice ask the first. "I guess that Ford F-150 tried to run the light. She T-boned the Mustang at full speed."

"Did the driver survive?" the second man asks.

"She's alert—drunk but alert. It's that rich brat, Angelina Firetti. Her family owns that fancy Italian restaurant in the Village district downtown." I hear him blow his breath. Angelina Firetti hit us? I must not have heard the conversation correctly. "I don't know about this young man, but it looks bad. The redhead is the only one I can reach through the mangled metal." The male voices fade away, and I don't hear them anymore. I squeeze my eyes closed, and their words keep ringing through my mind.

"Miss? Miss? Can you hear me?" a female voice suddenly penetrates my darkness. "Miss, can you tell me your name?"

"Tomorrow Williams," I mumble softly. I assume the lady heard me because she didn't ask again.

"And who's your friend? What's his name?" She sounds like she's shouting, and I wince.

"Caleb Logan. He's my best friend. Is he okay?" She continues untangling me from the seat belt but doesn't answer my question. "Is Caleb all right?" Again, no answer. "How come nobody is helping Caleb? He needs more help than I do."

I don't understand why she won't answer my question.

"I'll be right back, Miss." She disappears from my view.

"No, please, don't go!" My plea dissipates into the darkness. Sitting in the darkness, I continue my prayer that Caleb is okay and that we both walk away from this accident. Lights flash from emergency vehicles that have arrived, strobing red and blue lights across Caleb's face, which is covered in blood. I attempt to lean closer to him, but any movement causes excruciating pain in my right leg, and I cry out in pain.

"Tater?" Caleb stirs and whispers faintly. At first, I wondered if he was actually speaking or if it was my imagination. "You're hurt."

"Caleb?" I squirm in my seat, trying to reach him, but the twisted metal and seat belt have me pinned against the doorframe. "Oh my God, Caleb! You're alive!" Adrenaline surges through my veins. Caleb is alive. Thank you, God, Caleb is alive! "Caleb, can you move? Are you hurt? The paramedics are here trying to get us out." He doesn't respond, but I know I heard him speaking. *Caleb is alive!*

The female paramedic returns to continue working to dislodge me from the wreckage, but I push her away from me. "Please, help Caleb. He just said my name; he's conscious."

"Ms. Williams, please calm down," the woman says evenly. "We'll get you both out, I promise. But right now, I need you to calm down, so we can remove you from the car. Getting you out first will give us more room to help your friend. Do you understand?"

"But he needs more help than me. Please help him." I try to reach Caleb to touch him and let him know I heard him, but somehow, the steering wheel is between us. It isn't supposed to be there.

"Do you understand?" She repeats her question, and I nod in understanding.

The EMT sticks her head through the window and throws a blanket over our heads and Caleb's body. "Tomorrow, they are about to cut the frame of the car to peel the top off, so we can get you and Caleb out of the wreckage. It'll be loud, and sparks will fly, but this fireproof blanket will protect you and Caleb. I won't leave you, okay? I'm right by your side and won't let anything happen to you two." The piercing sound of metal against metal assaults my eardrums. Oh my God, they're cutting Caleb's car into pieces. His beautiful baby is being dissected piece by piece. He'll be heartbroken, and my heart breaks for him.

19

A flurry of activity swarms around me, until I'm nestled in the back of the ambulance with an EMT checking my vitals. Beyond the opened rear doors of the ambulance, a bright light glares over my head, and emergency vehicle lights flash. The mirage of sounds reminds me of the trauma that just happened. People are yelling orders at one another, metal screeches against metal, and glass breaks. I can only imagine what Caleb's car looks like. I hope they bring him into the same ambulance, so I can see for myself how he is. Time stands still inside the ambulance; the paramedic moves in slow motion, and nobody is talking to me. I desperately want to see Caleb.

"Will they bring my friend in the same ambulance?" I ask with hope in my voice.

"No, I'm sorry, sweetie," she says, with sympathy. "One person per transport."

"Do you know how he is?"

"No, I wish I did. You can ask once we get to the hospital. We're about to go now." The rear doors close, and the latch fastens from the outside. The overhead light continues to glow as the emergency vehicle starts. My caretaker continues to check me over, frowning as she examines my leg. The bruise on my leg is so dark it looks black.

"Is that dangerous? It looks nasty."

"They'll x-ray it when we get to the ER. At the very least, for the next few weeks, it'll hurt like the dickens when you try to walk."

"Will I be ok in time for prom?" Since I now have a date with Caleb, prom seems exciting. My stomach flutters at the thought.

"I don't think you'll be bedridden," she says, winking at me, and I smile sheepishly.

～

"TOMORROW!" Mom rips open the curtain that blocks my bed from the rest of the mayhem in the emergency room. "Oh, sweetheart, are you okay?" She rushes to my bedside and hugs me fiercely. "What happened? Is Caleb okay? I lost it when the police called, and so did your dad."

"We were coming home from Wine & Design in Apex. He had just asked me to prom, and a truck smashed into us." Tears start to leak from my eye sockets. "Nobody will tell me if Caleb is okay. Mom, do you know, or can you find out? Please."

"He's in surgery. They're setting his broken arm and wrapping ribs; he'll be pretty sore for a month or so," Dad said from across the room. "God was really protecting you two, because neither one of you received life-threatening injuries from the impact. The police officer from the scene told me that as fast as the driver of the truck was going, you two should have been dead."

"Thank God, he's alive," Mom said, echoing my thoughts exactly.

"You should be discharged in an hour or so, and the waiting room is filled with your friends. But Caleb won't be up to visitors right now," Mom informs me. "But we can ask his nurse to pass along the message that you're anxious to see him. Okay?"

"Yeah, okay." I want to see him, but I understand that I'll have to wait. "Does Today know what happened? Is she here?" Surely, she set aside her anger to be at the hospital for me. I know I would be here for her, no matter what we were arguing over. Mom and Dad exchange a look, and I know the answer before Mom speaks.

"She asked me to text and let her know if you two are okay," Mom said and sighs heavily. "She couldn't make it right now."

"She couldn't make it to see if her twin sister is dead or alive? That is below cold." I'm stunned that Today hates me that much. I thought it was sad that after the fire at school, she didn't care if I made it out of the cafeteria, but Caleb and I were just in a major wreck.

"I don't understand the riff between the two of you." Mom makes it sound more like a question than a statement.

"She thinks I wanted to go out with Troy." I can't believe I just spilled it to Mom. Well, it's part of my secret. I panic, waiting for the cascade of questions that are bound to follow. To my surprise, Mom doesn't expound on the subject; instead, she starts singing a song.

"Lord help the mister
that tries to come between me and my sister.
And, Lord help the sister,
that comes between me and my man."

. . .

"Really, Mom? You're singing?"

"Oh yes, that song was popular in the 1950s. No truer words were ever sung."

"That's all you're going to say on the matter?"

"Yes, you and your sister will have to work this out on your own."

"If you're finished singing, will you please find out about Caleb?"

"I'll stay with her, Vivian," my dad reassures my mom. "You go check on the boy. Nurses tend to respond better to women—you know, the motherly types." He winks at Mom, and I swear she blushes, and leaves the cubicle we are confined to.

"So, Half Pint, you two gave us quite a scare," Dad says and wipes a tear from his cheek. "We could have lost you."

"Dad, it wasn't Caleb's fault." I rise to defend my best friend. "That truck came from nowhere and smashed into us. I promise he did nothing wrong." I didn't want Mom and Dad to hold anything against Caleb. If anything, I distracted him. "I know, sweetheart, calm down. I spoke with the presiding officer from the scene. Apparently, there were eyewitnesses that saw her run the red light. the driver was Angelina Firetti. She totaled the truck she was driving. I believe the officers found alcohol in the vehicle. There was no fault on Caleb's part." Dad inhales deeply, and I can tell there's more he wants to say.

"Dad?"

"Uhm, well, the officer also said that from the impact and wreckage they witnessed when they arrived on the scene, he was positive it would be a recovery operation, and not a rescue," he pauses before continuing. "You and Caleb should not have made it out of that accident alive. Also, the injuries you two sustained are minimal compared to what should have been..."

I fall back on the uncomfortable hospital bed to soak in what Dad is telling me. We should be dead. We should not have come out of that accident alive.

"God protected you two for a purpose. I will be forever grateful he spared my baby girl and her—uhm, the son I never had." The weight of Dad's words settle over me. God saved me for a purpose.

"Dad, I need to settle things with Today, but in doing so, I may hurt her worse," I admit, feeling like a vulnerable little four-year-old telling him I broke Today's favorite doll.

"Is what you need to tell her the truth?"

"Yes," I mumble under my breath.

"The Bible tells us to speak the truth in love to become more like Him," Dad says and hugs me tightly. "Whatever you need to tell your sister, I'm sure you will feel much freer once it's out in the open."

Dad has a way of knowing things, even when I don't say a word. His words comfort me like being wrapped in a blanket that has just been removed from the dryer.

"I'm just not sure how to tell her...what I need to tell her." And I'm not sure she will believe me. Troy has told her so many lies, so much time has passed, and she has built so much hatred for me in her heart that my confession might be futile; but I have to tell Today the truth. The truth will set me free.

"Pray about it." Dad smiles sweetly. "The right words will come."

"Great news!" Mom pops her head around the curtain. "Caleb is going to be just fine. He has a broken arm, a dislocated shoulder, and some bumps and bruises, but it's going to be okay."

"Thank God." I exhale from the bottom of my lungs. I don't think I've been taking full breaths since the accident. Now that I know Caleb is okay, I can fully breathe. "Can I see him?"

"Unfortunately, no." Mom's smile turns upside down. "He's having an MRI done now, but all the x-rays were clear. They're keeping him overnight for observations, just as a precaution." That makes sense to me. "I'm sure he'll call you when he gets settled in his room. For now, young lady, you've been sprung from this joint. Let's go home."

"You have a waiting room full of friends here to see you," Mom informs me as she wheels me out of the ER treatment area.

"But, not my sister." A sob catches in my throat.

"Well, one of your sisters is here."

"Half-Pint!" Faith screams across the crowded waiting room and rushes to hug me. "You cared us half to death. Are you okay?" I tentatively hug her back; the adrenaline is wearing off, and I'm feeling the aftermath of being run over by a truck.

"I'll be okay," is all I manage to get out before all my friends swarm around me. Tammi, Jeremy, Bree, Carly, Wesley, Ashlynn, Austin, Faith, and Hunter have all been in the waiting room for hours. After being bombarded with questions for about twenty minutes, Mom suggests that she bring me home, so I can rest. I think it's a pretty good idea.

"Will someone let me know if they hear from Caleb?" I ask before Mom whisks me toward the ER entrance.

"Like you won't be the one first he calls when he gets his phone?" Bree winks at me and the rest of my friend group give knowing nods, agreeing with her.

～

"Hey, Tater, are you okay?" Caleb's voice on the other end of the line makes my heart soar. He sounds good, and that relieves my anxiety.

"Caleb, how are you? What did the doctors say? Are you okay?"

"I hurt in places I didn't know could hurt, but more importantly, how are you? I've been so worried about you. Are you hurt? The nurses wouldn't tell me anything, and the only thing Dad knew was that you had been released." He spewed out questions as fast as I did.

"I have the ugliest black bruise on my right thigh from being pinned against the doorframe, I have a few cuts from the glass, and I'm sore all over. It hurts to even move. I think I have bruised ribs or something," I inform him. "I'm so sorry about your Mustang. I can't believe they had to cut the top off to get us out, like they show on *COPS*."

"Yeah, Dad told me. That sucks. But you know what? It's just a car." Caleb tries to reassure me that it was just a car, but I know better. He loved that car and it was special for him and his dad. "I was more concerned about you. Are you sure you're okay?"

"Yes, I'll be fine." His concern for me touches my heart.

"I guess we won't be going to Austin's birthday cookout tomorrow. I'm sure your sister and Troy will miss our presence." Caleb starts to chuckle but stops abruptly. "Oh, goodness, I can't laugh. It hurts too badly."

"I can't believe she didn't even come to the hospital to see if we were okay. She just asked Mom to text her to let her know." The pain of my sister's absence floods my heart again.

"Hey, Tater, at least she asked, right?" I can hear him smiling on the other end. "That's a start. Granted, a small start, but a start nonetheless."

"I told Mom and Dad why Today is so mad at me, but not what he did to me."

"Oh wow, and how did that go over?"

"Mom started singing a song and said we need to work it out ourselves. Dad had more profound advice. He said to pray about it and then confess whatever secret I'm keeping to Today." I can feel the weight of that conversation on my chest. "You and I both know she'll never believe what I tell her. She's too brainwashed by Troy and the crap he has been feeding her."

"I think your dad is right, though. Pray about it. God has a way of working things out."

"Yeah, I guess," I respond weakly.

"I'm going to let you go for now, Tomorrow. The pain meds are kicking in, and I'm going to crash."

"Wow, what a crappy choice of words, Caleb."

"I told you not to make me laugh!"

"Oh, I'm so sorry!" I feel terrible now. But, hey, it was funny.

"Goodnight, Sweet Tater."

"Goodnight, Crash." Finally, after all these years, I have a good nickname for him.

SATURDAY DRAGS ON FOREVER. I watch the clock tick by, hour after hour, bored out of my skull. I don't want to call Caleb; he needs his rest after yesterday's accident, and all of my friends are at the birthday cookout Ashlynn planned for Austin. I hope it was a success, and Austin was surprised. Ashlynn put a lot of time, thought, effort, and money into the surprise party. I'm sorry I couldn't go, but I'm just not up to going anywhere right now. I'll be lucky to make it to school on Monday.

"Honey," Mom says, waking me at 6:00 p.m. "Tomorrow, honey, wake up."

"What's wrong? Is it Caleb?" I awaken with a start. My first thought was that Caleb collapsed or something worse. The trauma of the accident is still fresh in my brain.

"No, honey, Caleb is fine," she reassures me. "Today called a few minutes ago. She and Troy are on their way over, and they want to talk to the family."

"What does that have to do with me?" My reply is grumpy as I pull the covers back over my head. "Just let me sleep."

"She told me they want to speak to the whole family, which includes you and Faith. So, get up, honey. They'll be here any time now. Faith is already downstairs."

"What's this conversation about?"

"God only knows." Mom looks worried, and that's unnerving.

"Fine," is all I can muster, and Mom leaves my room. I dress in my Holly Springs High School hoodie, matching purple plaid sweatpants, and purple fuzzy slippers before heading downstairs to wait in the living room with Mom and Dad. I can only imagine what in the world those two are up to now. Mom and Dad look like they're wondering the same thing. This can't be good.

Fifteen minutes pass before Troy's truck roars into the driveway. My stomach clenches at the possibility of bad news arriving at the door. Mom is sitting in a wingback chair by the fireplace and Dad takes his position standing behind her. I sit on the couch with my socked feet tucked underneath me, hugging Penelope to my chest. She's part of the family after all. When the two of them enter the house, Today looks nervous, and Troy looks cocky. I have a feeling they're going to tell us that they are foregoing college and moving away. I wouldn't put it past these two self-centered people. It's all about what they want, regardless of who they hurt.

"Hi, Mom, Dad, and Faith," Today beams as she kisses our parents hello. She turns to me and practically spits out my name. "Tomorrow."

"Mr. and Mrs. Williams," Troy greets Mom and Dad formally. *What is up with these two?*

"Come in and sit down," Mom says, sounding very uncomfortable, which is out of character for her. She keeps fidgeting with her hair as she shows Today and Troy to the loveseat across from Faith and me. *Can we say 'awkward'?*

"So, what's this family meeting all about?" Dad cuts right to the chase. *You go, Dad*, I think to myself.

Today and Troy look at each other with toothy smiles before Today explains, "Mom. Dad. We've waited for a while to tell you our news, to make sure everything was progressing as it should and we've decided now is the time."

"And that 'news' is?" Dad says in a snarky voice while making air quotes above his head.

Today giggles slightly before announcing, "We're pregnant!"

Mom gasps. Dad rubs his temples while closing his eyes. I pick my jaw off the floor, and Faith mumbles several expletives under her breath.

"You're what?" Mom stutters, clasping her hand over her mouth.

"I'm eight weeks pregnant!" Today bounces in her seat, clearly ecstatic about the situation.

I'm speechless. How stupid can my sister be? She's just turned eighteen, only been married a few short months, and hasn't graduated high school, yet she's excited to be pregnant. I would be scared out of my ever-loving mind.

Ding! Dong! The doorbell chimes, breaking through the shock that fills the living room. Nobody makes a move to answer the door.

Stumbling to my feet, I numbly walk into the foyer and open the door. I come face to face with two uniformed police officers. Am I in the twilight zone or what? Why are there cops at the door at the most inappropriate time ever?

"Can I help you?" I stammer.

"Good evening, Miss. We're looking for Troy Whitaker. We were told we could find him here. Is that correct?" The taller officer speaks; the shorter one stands behind him, looking stoic.

"I'm Troy Whitaker." Troy stands in the entryway of the living room to my left. "Can I help you, Officer?"

"Troy Allan Whitaker, you are under arrest for the rape of Aubry Phillips." The police officer steps toward Troy with handcuffs at the ready.

20

"You have the wrong guy," Troy stammers, but I see sweat beads forming on his forehead. I can tell he's lying through his teeth. "I don't know an Aubry Phillips."

Dad takes a large swallow of his brandy. Mom gasps and lowers herself into the wingback chair by the fireplace. Today turns green, and my eyes bug out. I thought Today's pregnancy announcement was as bad as this evening could get. Boy, was I wrong?

"Yes, you do," I say, stepping forward boldly. "You know Bree quite well. Her name is actually Aubry, but she goes by Bree. Oh my God, you raped Bree?"

"Oh, shut up, Tomorrow!" Today snaps at me. "You stay out of this!"

"You shut up! Bree is my friend!" I scream back at her. "You need to control this loser of a husband you have. I guarantee Bree isn't the first girl he's assaulted!"

"What the hell does that mean?"

Faith jumps from the sofa to stand between Today and

me, keeping us apart. "Okay, you two, calm down. Emotions are running high."

"Now, girls, this isn't the time." Dad calls a ceasefire in the den before I spill what Troy did to me at Homecoming. "We have to deal with the situation at hand."

"This is bullshit," Troy protests, but is ignored by the officers making the arrest.

"Troy Whitaker," the shorter officer says and steps toward Troy. "Place your hands behind your back, sir."

Troy does as he is told, and the police officer clicks the shiny metal handcuffs into place. "You have the right to remain silent. Anything you say can and will be used against you in a court of law. You have the right to an attorney. If you cannot afford an attorney, one will be provided for you. Do you understand the rights I have just read to you? With these rights in mind, do you wish to speak to me?"

"Not without my lawyer," he says before turning to Today, "Babe, call my parents and tell my dad to have Jarvis meet me at the police station."

Today wraps an arm around her midsection, presumably to protect the baby growing in her belly, and nods. My heart breaks for her; she looks so small and frail—not to mention terrified. Troy is an ass, but she obviously loves the jerk. I've spent all these months trying to protect her from what Troy did to me, and now he ends up hurting her worse by what's unfolding before our very eyes. Mom is crying softly in the corner, but I'm not sure if her tears are from the pregnancy announcement or the rape charge.

Today calls after Troy as the police officer escorts him from the house, "I love you, babe."

"I love you, too. It'll be okay, just call my dad and take care of you and the baby." Wow, was that concern from Troy for his wife and child? I didn't think he was capable of loving anyone but himself.

The heavy entry door closes behind Troy with a loud thud that reverberates throughout the foyer. An eerie hush settles over the house as nobody speaks. Shock moves through the family, until Today bursts into tears as she collapses onto the leather sofa, breaking the frozen hold we are all trapped in. Mom rushes to her side to comfort her. Faith is uncharacteristically quiet. Dad pulls his cell phone from his shirt pocket and announces that he'll call Mr. Whitaker for Today. I don't want to feel sorry for her, but I do. She's my twin sister and is carrying my niece or nephew. But what about Bree? Troy raped her? What about what he did to me? What about all these months she has refused to speak to me because of his lies? Could Troy be the father of the child Bree thought she was carrying? Wouldn't she have told me it was Troy? There are so many questions without answers, and each question leads to *more* questions.

Mom and Dad drive Today to the police station, leaving me alone in the house with my thoughts.

I don't know who to call first: Caleb, Faith, Bree, or Tammi. Originally, I opted for Caleb because he is my 'go-to' person but think better of it. He's pretty banged up from the accident and mourning the loss of his car, so I decided to hold off talking to him about it. Instead, I choose to text Sierra. My mind races a million miles an hour after the events of the day. Because of the accident, I realize life can change on a dime. Here it is, only twenty-four hours later, and the coin has flipped again.

TOMORROW: *Are you sitting down?*
  Sierra: *Uh oh, what happened?*

Tomorrow: *Today and Troy stopped by—Today announced she's pregnant.*

Sierra: Holy Crow, *how did that go over with your parents? I mean, they're married, but still...*

Tomorrow: *Well, before anybody could react, the cops showed up and arrested Troy.*

Sierra: *For what??*

Tomorrow: *Supposedly raping my friend Bree.*

Sierra: *What?? Bree?? When?*

Tomorrow: *I'm not sure. I spoke to her yesterday, and she didn't mention anything. Of course, I had just been in an accident, but she sounded normal. So, I have no idea.*

A FEW MINUTES pass before Sierra's next text comes through.

SIERRA: *Bree is your friend who had the pregnancy scare, right?*

Tomorrow: *Yeah, thank God it was a false alarm.*

Sierra: *And she wouldn't tell you who the father was?*

Tomorrow: *That's right. What are you getting at?*

Sierra: *Nothing, I guess. Forget I mentioned it.*

Tomorrow: *Spill it, Sierra.*

Sierra: *Don't you think it's a little too coincidental that Bree thought she was pregnant and then accused Troy of rape.*

Tomorrow: *You think Troy could have been the father?*

Sierra: *It was just a thought. My brain goes into overdrive sometimes. I have been accused of being a conspiracy theorist on more than one occasion. LOL*

I DON'T MENTION it to Sierra, but I do remember the day of the fire at school when Bree was acting very strangely and staring at Troy and Today across the cafeteria. I wonder if Sierra is on to something or if I'm getting caught up in her wild imagination.

TOMORROW: *I had just about resigned myself to telling Today what really happened the night of Homecoming. I don't think she would have believed me, but it's been eating away at me all these months. I feel stuck in this limbo and unable to move out of it.*

Sierra: *As I've told you several times now, you need to unburden the load you're carrying. It's a vital step to healing and moving on with your life. It doesn't matter if she believes you or not. The point is, you need to stop harboring the guilt and shame of this secret, even though those emotions aren't warranted in this situation. You did NOTHING to deserve these emotions.*

Tomorrow: *I can't tell her now. She's going through enough without me stacking on another trauma.*

Sierra: *If the accusations are true, you must tell her now. Your testimony could be substantial to the investigation and prosecution. I know you don't want your sister hurting more than she is now, but you have to consider your mental health, too. You have to be able to heal and move on from that night. If you don't, you'll never be whole again. That isn't fair to you. You were the victim, Tomorrow. Pray about it. You need to do what is best for you.*

Tomorrow: *Okay, I will. Thank you. I couldn't have made it this far without you.*

Sierra: *I'm always here.*

Tomorrow: *I will keep you updated on "As the Williams Family Turns".*

Sierra: *You do that. TTYL*

· · ·

It's DARK OUTSIDE, and the streetlights cast an ominous glow through the mist. It must have rained, and I missed it. After drawing my shades to block out the night, I get Penelope from her cage and pad across the hall to Faith's room. As I approach Faith's door, I hear her softly crying. It isn't like Faith to cry. She's always the strong one of the three sisters. I decide to take Pen into Faith's room. Even if she doesn't want to talk, she can at least cuddle with her baby. As a bonus, Penelope is a wonderful listener.

Tapping lightly on her door, I listen closely for her to grant entry. "Come in," Faith answers almost inaudibly.

Her room is dark; the only light is from a small flickering candle nightlight beside her bed. It's boho chic, complete with a round handwoven rug in the center and a hanging chair with tassels in the corner. Her room is cozy and comfortable. I miss coming in here when she's away at school. I know it's only a matter of time before she takes her stuff and no longer comes home.

"Faith?" I question and lay Penelope in her lap. "Are you okay?"

"Hi, Pen," she says, as she nuzzles the skunk's neck with her nose. "Thanks for bringing her in. How did you know what I needed?" Faith sits up in her bed and leans against the headboard. Patting the mattress beside her, she indicates for me to climb in between her and the wall. I remember doing this countless times when I was little. I was afraid of thunder, and Faith always made me feel safe tucked in her bed.

"I figured you needed your snuggle buddy."

"Yeah, I think I'm still in shock, on top of being sad, mad, and resentful of Today." She speaks more to Penelope than to me. Sometimes, it's easier to admit true feelings when talking to Pen. Lord knows I've laid bare my soul to her on numerous occasions.

"Resentful? Why?" I didn't expect Faith to be harboring resentment toward our sister.

"She's so selfish! She stole all the things that should have been mine." Faith sniffles into Penelope's fur. "I'm the oldest. I was supposed to be the first married. I should be having the first grandchild. The spotlight should be on me, not Today."

I hear the pain in her voice. I understand where she's coming from. I, too, have felt betrayed by our sister. I had never lied to Today before the night of Homecoming. We always knew we had each other's back, but instead of asking me what happened or defending my honor, she believed Troy and turned her back on me.

"I'm so sorry, Faith." I lean my head on her shoulder and start petting Pen along with Faith. Penelope relishes the attention. She's a spoiled baby.

"Thanks, I appreciate it," she says and turns to me with a very serious look on her face, her brow creased. "Something you said tonight has been bothering me, Morrow. I can't get it out of my mind."

"What is it?" I ask, terrified of her response.

"When you and Today were screaming at each other downstairs, you said you guaranteed Bree wasn't the first girl Troy has assaulted. What did you mean by that?"

"I was just mad, that's all," I stammer while picking at the strings on Faith's quilt, which Mom made her for her sixteenth birthday.

"I'm not buying that, Tomorrow. You've been distant, preoccupied, and short-tempered for quite a while. You've started to tell me something twice. The first was at Thanksgiving, and then again on your birthday, but both times we were interrupted. I've been waiting for you to reach out to me, but you haven't. Now it's time to fess up. Did something happen that you aren't telling me?"

"Well, the CliffsNotes version is that the night of Homecoming, Troy tried to rape me. He didn't succeed, but he did enough damage to scar me for life." The tears I've managed to keep in check for the past few months begin to flow. Oddly, I don't feel that I've backslid, but instead, that admitting the truth to Faith is freeing. I don't feel the same shame I did when I told the truth to Tammi or Sierra. Probably because Faith is my sister.

"Oh, dear Lord, Tomorrow. Did you report it to the police? What did Today do about it?" Faith sits up in alarm.

"No, I didn't tell anybody for a long time. I tried to protect Today because I didn't want to hurt her. Only Tammi and Caleb know the truth."

"Why didn't you tell Today? She has a right to know."

"Because I thought he was just drunk until he sent me a text with a picture from that night in his truck saying I belong to him."

"Oh My God! How did he get a picture? I don't understand."

"He has a dashcam in his truck. I guess he records the inside of his truck, not over the hood." Shame starts to creep in, but I push it down. I'm clean and blameless in Christ and have nothing to be ashamed of. Sierra is teaching me these truths.

"But I still don't understand; how did this cause a rift between you and Today? This is Troy's doing; why is she mad at you?"

"Because he showed the picture to Today and told her I came on to him, that I have been after him for months, and she believed it. She's blind to the true nature of him. When they got married," I huff, "she told me that he was hers now and I would never have him. Things are so twisted, Faith. I held all of this in until Caleb's aunt hooked me up with Sierra. She's a trained Stephen Minister. We meet once a week to talk, and she's helping me realize that I'm not soiled, I'm not to blame, and I'm not damaged goods. She points out biblical principles and scripture to help me cope. I've come a long way. I finally had the strength to stand up to Today and tell her the truth...until tonight. I can't believe she's pregnant, and Bree accused him of rape, and that it all came to light within minutes of each other." I inhale a deep breath after baring my soul, and Faith exhales in disbelief.

"Sweetie, why didn't you come to me? Why didn't you let me help you carry this burden? I'm your big sister, it's my job." She wraps me in a warm embrace, and I feel safe. I've carried this secret from my family for so long that I assumed this weight was a permanent part of my existence, and I would have to learn to live with it.

After a few minutes of silent contemplation on both our parts, Faith speaks up. "Do you think he raped Bree?"

I filled her in on Bree's recent pregnancy scare, how she refused to tell me who the would-be father was, and about her staring at Troy before the fire at school. Thinking back, I've noticed her odd behavior around Troy and Today, but didn't add two and two together to equal four. I've been too wrapped up in myself to give much thought to others.

"I wouldn't put it past him. If it did happen against her will, I would bet my life that there's a recording of it on his dashcam. Apparently, he gets off on video of him with girls." The thought turns my stomach. He's one sick individual.

"Well, then we need to get that camera and pull the footage and expose that bastard for who he really is." Faith's ire is up, and there's no stopping her now. Her determination emboldens me. *Thank you, God, for my big sister. You knew how much I would need her before I did*, I think to myself.

"How in the world are we going to do that?" I ask incredulously.

"I have no earthly idea, but I know someone who does," Faith says, gleaming with deviousness. I've seen that look before. There have been too many pranks played on our parents over the years and I know she's up to something.

"Who?"

"Hunter, of course." she giggles. I'm glad she isn't sad anymore, even if we are talking about how to expose Troy. Whatever it takes, right? "He's a mastermind with electronics. I have no doubt he can figure out how to tap into Troy's dashcam. I'm going to call him right now." Faith grabs her cell phone from the nightstand and taps out a text to Hunter. I overheard her on the phone with Hunter shortly after Mom and Dad left with Today for the police station, so he's already filled in on the details of the night's events.

"No way," Faith exclaims, pulling me from my reverie. "God is smiling on us right now."

"What are you talking about?" Sometimes Faith says random thoughts that make sense only in her head.

"Hunter said all we have to do is get the memory card from the dashcam and copy it to your laptop." She sounds like we just won the lottery. "And isn't his truck still here? I'm sure Today rode with Mom and Dad."

Panic fills my chest, and I don't feel like I can get enough oxygen into my lungs. My earlier confidence quickly fades into a vapor. The prospect of seeing the video of that night is too much. I hadn't thought this thing through this far. I don't think I can do this. "I don't want to see that video, if it's there, Faith. I can't relive that night. I'm just starting to get over it. Please, don't make me do this." I start to cry, pull my knees to my chest, and curl into the corner of the bed against the wall. "I can't do it, Faith."

"Oh, honey, it's ok. I'll get the memory card and find the footage, if it's still there, okay?" She squeezes my hand reassuringly. "You let your big sister handle this." Before I could wipe my tears, she was gone. I heard her exit the house through the front door, and before I knew it, she was running back up the stairs and into her room. Just as she closed her bedroom door, the garage door opened. Mom and Dad were back.

"Oh my God, that was close!" Faith exclaimed to me.

"Yeah, how would you have explained being in Troy's truck?" I sure hope the dome light had turned off before the family turned into the driveway. We'll have to play dumb if asked about it.

Faith is already sitting at her laptop and browsing the content of the memory card. "This is perfect. Each day has its own folder on the card. I don't have to watch hours of traffic or things I don't want to see. What was the date of the Homecoming Dance?" She asked me without taking her eyes off the screen. I stand off to her left side, leaning against the closet door, not wanting to accidentally see anything from those files.

"October 6th."

"Got it."

It didn't take long for her to locate the correct folder. I excuse myself to the bathroom while she does her thing. I'm not sure if there is sound on the recordings, and I don't want to risk hearing anything from that night. I decide to take a shower and let the water drown out any conversation on that memory card. Twenty-five minutes later, once all the hot water is depleted, I emerge wrapped in one of Faith's bathrobes, my hair up in a towel on my head, barefooted.

She's sitting on her bed, scrolling through Facebook on her phone when I walk in.

"You okay?" she asks, sounding worried.

"Yeah, I'm okay. Did you find it?"

"I did. I copied it to your laptop and then transferred it to a flash drive." Her smile was smug. "Don't worry; I deleted it from your hard drive, so you won't accidentally open it. Then I took the flash drive and gave it to Today."

"What? Why?" Oh, this could be bad. I'm not sure what I thought we were going to do with the evidence, but I wasn't expecting it to happen so quickly.

"I told her that she never should have trusted Troy in the first place and believed the lies he told her, especially about you. Then I tossed the flash drive and the memory card on her desk and walked out. I must say, it was quite satisfying."

"Did you watch it?" I feel the old shame creeping back into my soul until I remember Sierra telling me that shame is a lie of Satan and to reject it. So, I do, or at least try.

"Only until you pushed him off of you. That was enough for me to see to know it was the right file." She patted the mattress again, indicating for me to sit with her. "Tomorrow, I'm so sorry you had to go through that, and I'm sorry you've been dealing with this on your own. I'm grateful that you had Tammi and Caleb to help you through it, though."

"Sierra was a huge help, too. I told her things that I wasn't able to share with Caleb and Tammi, for obvious reasons. She always gave me words of wisdom from the Bible that have helped me heal. I owe her a lot." I realize now how much Sierra has helped me over the past few weeks. She's a blessing.

A soft knock interrupts our conversation, "Faith? Tomorrow? May I please come in?" It's Today.

"Of course, Sweet Pea, come in." Faith looks at me and winks.

Today takes a seat at the desk and stares at the floor. She has the flash drive and memory card clasp in a tight grip in her right hand. Her eyes are red and swollen. Her face is wet from freshly fallen tears, and she bounces on one knee like she's about to come out of her skin. Abruptly, she stills, takes a deep breath, and faces me for the first time in months without loathing behind her eyes. "Morrow, I'm so, so sorry for how I've treated you. I'm sorry I actually thought you would do that to me...I mean, go after Troy. He fed me lie after lie about you, things I should have known weren't true. I'm so sorry, Tomorrow." She begins to sob, and all my anger melts away. I leap off the bed and wrap her in the biggest hug I've ever given. I love my sister, *both* of my sisters, more than anything in the world. *Thank you, God, that I have her back*, I thought to myself.

"It's okay, Today. I love you, and I forgive you." I hold her tightly for a couple of minutes before sitting back on the bed. Faith squeezes my hand again. "So, what do we do now?"

"I was looking at the dates of the videos on the memory card that Troy saved. They coincide with the dates and times I had dance class. He never would come in and watch me practice; now I know why. He and Bree have been seeing each other for weeks. The sex seemed consensual, from what I saw." She hung her head, letting her long red hair shield her face, before continuing. "Until yesterday, after Ashlynn's party. I went to the apartment to lay down, and he 'went to the store,'" she said in air quotes. "He met Bree. They fought because he hadn't left me yet..." she trails off, crying again.

"Oh, my goodness, Today." Faith says, embracing my

older twin, and rocking her side-to-side like a baby. Actually, I realize she *is* like a fragile baby.

"I think the police need to see this," she says, holding up the memory card. "Morrow Bear, will you take me to the police station so I can give it to the detective working the case?"

"Absolutely. Let me get my keys," I say and race toward the door.

"Uhm, put some clothes on first," Faith suggests, and out of pure emotion and adrenaline, we all laugh.

"Good idea."

EPILOGUE

"You look beautiful, Tomorrow." Caleb blushes slightly as we step off the porch into the warm late May evening. Since he rarely calls me Tomorrow, I know the compliment is sincere. I chose a deep teal, Cinderella style ballgown for the prom. I'm thrilled Caleb likes the look. I was a little worried because the latest trends feature skintight dresses that leave nothing to the imagination. But I want to feel like a princess tonight, and this gown is perfect.

"You don't look so bad yourself, Mr. Logan." Now I'm the one blushing, but dang, the boy looks good in a black tuxedo.

He takes my hand and leads me down the walkway to his new black Jeep Wrangler, which has a hard top, along with all the bells and whistles. It's a beauty. I slide into the passenger seat, enjoying the smell of leather and the buttery softness of the material. Caleb trots around the front of the Jeep and hops in the driver's side. "Ready to go, M'lady?" He winks at me and grins.

"Most definitely," I assure him and click my seatbelt into

place. He does the same, starts the engine, and the Jeep comes to life. He has the radio playing softly; since the accident, he no longer drives with the music blaring, and I'm thankful for that. "I can't believe we'll be graduating in ten days. It seems like we just started kindergarten yesterday."

"I don't know about you, but kindergarten seems a lot farther in my past than yesterday, Tater Tot. I didn't think graduation would ever get here." We drive in silence for a while, and I think about what he just said. It's true; time moves differently for different people. Life experiences, the ups and downs of growing older, losses and successes all shape our future, and we each arrive at our future when God ordains us. To me, that's a comforting thought.

"I wish Today was here," I say out loud when my mind flips to my sister living in Wyoming with our aunt and uncle. She is three and a half months pregnant and finishing her senior year online. I don't blame her for leaving Holly Springs while the legal system goes through the motions of Troy's sentencing. She'll be back before the baby is born. I can't wait to be Aunt Morrow.

"I know you do. I actually miss her, too." he chuckles. "I heard Troy plead guilty to a lesser charge than rape."

"Yeah, sexual assault. It's only a misdemeanor, instead of a felony. I don't think that's fair but have to accept it, I guess. Today has already filed for a separation. In North Carolina, they have to be living separately for one year and one day before filing for divorce. Isn't that weird?" I never understood that law, but it is what it is.

"That's crazy, both the plea bargain and the divorce law, but that's North Carolina for you." He makes a right into the school's parking lot and finds a parking space but chooses to take up two spaces. "I don't want the paint to get scratched," he says. He must have read my mind.

"I got a text from Bree this morning. She wants a ton of pictures of everybody at the prom. I promised her I would video chat her from inside."

"How is she?"

"She's lonely in New Jersey, and her folks don't really trust her now since she lied to them every time she was out with Troy. I can't say that I blame them." I understand why they moved her away from Holly Springs, but I miss her.

Caleb shuts off the engine, and we sit under the streetlamp's glow for a few minutes. He takes my hand in his and squeezes gently before he speaks. "We never really talked about the night of the accident," he says shaky, "and there's very little I remember about it."

"You were pretty banged up, Caleb," I reassured him. "I wouldn't expect you to remember anything."

"I do remember one thing, though," he said, his inhale sharp. "I remember waking up to your voice saying my name. I thought I was dead or dying, but I clearly remember hearing you say that you love me. Do you remember that?"

Staring at my hand in his, I respond in a low voice, "Yes, I remember."

He tilts my chin with his crooked index finger until I look directly into his beautiful eyes. "I love you too, Tomorrow Williams. I have since the day I gave you the ant farm." With that, he leans in and softly kisses my lips.

ACKNOWLEDGMENTS

To my husband, Steve (aka Douche Canoe), I love you. Thank you for always supporting my writing and asking *DAILY*, "Are you writing?". My mom always told me I could do anything if I put my mind to it. To my twin sister, Tammi Brock, for giving unconditional love. My adult twins, Josh and Amy, for understanding, when I ignored them because my mind was in Holly Springs when they were talking. SORRY! Admiral Nelson, you know why. Aspen Blake, thank you for all your hard work editing my book, which was a trainwreck without your help. God for inspiring me when my mind was blank. To you, my reader, for the love and support you have given me since the release of my first book. I hope someday you visit the town of Holly Springs in North Carolina. You will fall in love with it just as I have.

ANGELINA BOOK 3

Upcoming from T.A. Perret's
Holly Springs Book Series,
An excerpt from
Angelina
Holly Springs Book Series 3
Coming late fall 2025

PROLOGUE

"Jackson Bennett, you no good piece of crap. Call me back right now!" Angelina Firetti screamed into her cell phone before throwing it into the passenger seat of her dad's truck. She knew she shouldn't have taken his vehicle; his midnight blue, loaded to the gills with all the bells and whistles extended cab truck, was her dad's pride and joy. He wouldn't have allowed her to take it if she had asked, especially with a bottle of liquor in her possession...so she didn't. Angelina's candy apple red convertible Mercedes Benz was in the shop, having the black canvas top replaced again after she punched a hole in it after another fight with Jackson. She needed to find Jackson and was almost sure she knew where to find him. He was probably camped out at Thanks-A-Latte, gawking at Amy Bergen. Did he think she was stupid? She had seen Jackson staring at Amy when he thought she wasn't looking. Amy, with her sparkling blue eyes and cute bobbed red hair. The only thing she was missing were freckles, for God's sake. Angelina spat. Amy disgusted her. She would punch Amy out if she weren't her best friend's younger sister.

"Who the hell does he think is breaking up with *me*? "Angelina slurred into the windshield, pointing at the darkness on the other side. "With Me? There are a thousand guys at Holly Springs High that would kill to pick up the Kleenex I blew my nose in, but Jackson dumps *me*. I don't think so!" She grabbed the bourbon she had stolen from her parent's liquor cabinet and gulped another long drink from the now half-empty bottle.

The yellow lines on the highway zigzagged in front of her, but amazingly, she managed to keep the truck between the two stripes. She was only about a mile from the coffee shop where Amy worked and was positive she would find Jackson there. She kept driving. She flipped her long black hair over her left shoulder and glanced in the rearview mirror. Her dark chocolate-brown eyes were filled with anger, causing the gold flecks to be more prominent than usual. The bloodshot whites made her look evil. *Good*, she thought. *Jackson needs to be afraid when I catch him with her.*

Angelina's cell phone rang in the seat beside her, shattering the silence in the cab. Jackson's face appeared on the display. "It's about time!" she yelled, reaching across the console to retrieve the device. "It's about damn time, Jackson!"

When she grabbed the phone, the truck veered to the right, causing Angelina to hit the gravel on the side of the road. Intuitively, she jerked the wheel to the left to get back on the pavement, but in her drunken state, she overcorrected. The last thing Angelina saw as she blew through the red stoplight was a dark-colored Mustang just behind the truck's hood before she broadsided the muscle car at full speed.

Made in the USA
Columbia, SC
29 September 2024

43262101R00129